REVENGE AND FORGIVENESS

REVENGE

AND

Forgiveness

AN ANTHOLOGY OF POEMS

EDITED BY

Patrice Vecchione

HENRY HOLT AND COMPANY • NEW YORK

Henry Holt and Company, LLC
Publishers since 1866
115 West 18th Street
New York, New York 10011
www.henryholt.com

Henry Holt is a registered trademark of
Henry Holt and Company, LLC

Compilation and Introduction copyright © 2004
by Patrice Vecchione
All rights reserved.
Distributed in Canada by H. B. Fenn and Company Ltd.

Library of Congress Cataloging-in-Publication Data
Revenge and forgiveness : an anthology of poems /
edited by Patrice Vecchione
p.   cm.
Includes index.
Summary: A collection of nearly sixty poems dealing
with revenge and forgiveness, plus suggested readings about
each contributing poet.
1. Children's poetry.   2. Children's poetry—Translations into
English.   3. Poetry—Collections.   4. Poetry—Translations into
English.   5. Revenge in literature.   6. Forgiveness in literature.
[1. Poetry—Collections.   2. Revenge—Poetry.   3. Forgiveness—
Poetry.]   I. Vecchione, Patrice.
PN6109.97.R48 2004   808.81'9353—dc22
2003056631

ISBN 0-8050-7376-0 / EAN 978-0-8050-7376-8
First Edition—2004 / Design by Debbie Glasserman
Printed in the United States of America on acid-free paper. ∞
1   3   5   7   9   10   8   6   4   2

ACKNOWLEDGMENTS

Thank you to Laura Godwin, Kate Farrell, Marion Silverbear, Charlotte Raymond, Alyssa Raymond, Morton Marcus, Michael Stark, the entirely helpful reference librarians at the Monterey Public Library. For taking ideas and running with them, thanks to Jeanne McCombs and the Monterey Library Poetry Circle; Janis O'Driscoll and the Santa Cruz County Libraries for their support of the teen writing workshops and teen writer Daniel Campos; Lynn Larsen and her Pacific Grove High School students, including those students whose poems appear in the introduction: Rilke Allen, Jade Clark-Wilson, Jono Johnson, Evan McCombs, Ben Phillips, and Sarah Prochaska.

FOR ELIZABETH, WITH LOVE

CONTENTS

REVENGE AND FORGIVENESS

LIVING WITH REVENGE AND FORGIVENESS

One doesn't have to look far to find examples of revenge and forgiveness—just read the morning paper, live your daily life, and there they are. We've all felt angry and said things we later wish we hadn't. The revenge we take with our words may be momentarily empowering, until the impact of what we've said hits home. Consider the weight of vengeful words spoken against someone you care for. Forgiveness, on the other hand, can give us tremendous relief, make us feel, momentarily, pretty sublime. There's a rush to being forgiven, but there is also a way in which it can feel embarrassing. To receive forgiveness means we're also being called to task, and sometimes, I don't know about you, but I'd rather my act of meanness just be forgotten or ignored.

Revenge and forgiveness are both the result of something else—a wrong committed or perceived. Each is a way of responding. Though revenge may often take the most obvious form—such as a friend starting a false rumor—it can also be subtle—that friend just doesn't return your calls anymore. Revenge can take the form of a rather small action or a couple of delicately worded phrases that weaken the ground you're standing on.

Years ago my mother lay in a coma, dying. There had been years of fracture between us that had worn me sad and bitter. On one of her last days, I closed the curtains in her hospital room, then got up onto the bed, bent myself close to her, held her face in my hands, and said the words that had buried themselves inside me, the ones I needed to release to forgive her part of the feud that kept us apart for an awfully long time. The years of anger between us that had wedged themselves forcefully against me melted. There weren't many words. Just enough. Sometimes forgiveness does more for the one giving it than for the one in receipt.

In our world, on a large scale, you can turn in any number of directions and see evidence of revenge being taken. Some say the terrorist attacks of September 11 were acts of revenge against our country. And the response of our country, is that justice or revenge? We've all been changed by what happened. The tragedy of September 11 inspired this book. I wanted to create a tangible forum, a book to hold in our hands, to help frame and think about not just terrorism, but who we are as individuals and who we are as a country. How do we live with what overwhelms and frightens us? This book has been gestating in me for all this time. Finding these poems was like turning little lights on to illumine the dark. How can beauty be made out of ugliness and fear? Can it rise from ash?

POETRY IN ACTION

I brought a number of the poems in this anthology to several high-school classes. One of the best ways I know to find answers is to write poems. Even just writing my questions down can transform them. I read a number of the poems from this collection to the students. Then we discussed them, and the students wrote their own poetry on subjects connected to revenge and forgiveness. Here are some of their words.

Rilke writes:
> When I hate something it hurts,
> it deepens into a realization:
> I don't hate it.
> I hate everything I cannot grasp.
> Nothing wants to go untouched.

Sarah writes:
> Sometimes even when I yell
> I know it's stupid,
> but she is stupid too,
> so I can justify it.

From Jade:
> . . . What he did to her, broke
> her heart.
> She gave it to him,
> yet he took it away.
> She waits for him to give it back.
> But he is selfish
> and wants to keep it for his own . . .

And from Evan:

> I want to scoop up hate from the earth and throw it in their faces. A bullet fired gives satisfaction until it hits. . . . Plains of icy dread envelop me. What is it I want? Can my hungry flames withstand the ice of regret? Is the bullet worth the blood? How can I tell? Who can tell me?

Ben asks:

> What is peace?
> Is it the opposite of violence?
> Or is it just tolerable violence?

And lastly, Daniel writes:

> For love to be a curse,
> then hate must be a blessing.

Anger, blame, and revenge are aspects of human nature. Understanding, compassion, and forgiveness are also part of who we are. Poetry, as well, is our nature. To speak is a basic human need. Art can intimately show us ourselves and one another. When writing freely, we can express who we really are, what we truly think, revealing even the parts we don't understand. Poetry that is candid and real can help us to see others as ourselves. That brings us to empathy—if we see ourselves as similar to one another—vulnerable and in need of love, we may be compelled to find innovative ways to respond to the contradictory complexities of our world. Thus, art can be a form of healing. It narrows the gaps between us.

In these pages you'll find art made of revenge and forgiveness. The first poem, a song from a Quechan myth, sets the stage for this collection—"My heart, you might pierce it and take it." We do hold that power when we love and are loved. We're best when we don't forget it. For most of us, experiences of revenge and forgiveness begin in childhood, at home or with friends. The early poems here look at our foundations, including work by Kenneth Patchen, Molly Peacock, and Louise Glück.

Some poets take revenge with their writing. D. H. Lawrence said, "I like to write when I feel spiteful; it's like having a good sneeze." On the other side, Ezra Pound writes a poem to Walt Whitman as an apology for having taken writing-revenge against Whitman in the past.

There are poems that explore the political stories behind revenge and forgiveness—Victor H. Bausch writes about the Vietnam War and the way it scarred him. Muriel Rukeyser turns her attention to World Wars I and II, and talks about how necessary writing was to her during that time. Semezdin Mehmedinovic writes about a child in the Bosnian war who takes up a machine gun and kills, an act quite far from the experiences most people are familiar with.

The way we respond when it comes to romance is often startling. We may say and do things we never thought we would. Love and vulnerability can push us to the edge. In a love relationship, poet Ellen Bass finds herself closer to murder than she'd have thought possible. Mariahadessa

Ekere Tallie's poem is a note in the voice of a woman scorned. Gary Young shows us anger in a surprising way. Lilla Cabot Perry doesn't want forgiveness; she wants anger to remain because it reminds her that she is alive. It takes one word only to bring Sandra Cisneros to forgiveness, one word said just so.

You'll find poems about the anger and resulting revenge we feel and take not only against others, but against ourselves. Ultimately isn't that where cruelty begins—when we see ourselves as not lovable? It's difficult to respect and have regard for others if we feel bad about who we are. Tim Reynolds writes hatefully of his own heart, and Cecilia Woloch describes the reclamation of her sense of her own beauty, a kind of forgiveness.

In his poem, "Any Lover to Any Beloved," Faiz Ahmed Faiz writes, "After this meeting / we will know even better what we have lost." That may be said about this book, too. I hope these poems will help you deepen your understanding of human nature—of our strengths and foibles. When we take revenge against another, we lose some of our innocence, some of our humanity. Perhaps when you've read these poems, you, too, will know more clearly what has been lost to us as citizens of the United States and as members of the larger world. That's not a bad thing. Robert Frost once wrote, "The best way out is always through." To reclaim and redefine identity and to move forward, one must know where one stands, who one is—as an individual, as a country, as a world.

Naomi Shihab Nye, in her poem "Jerusalem" writes, "I'm not interested in / who suffered the most. / I'm interested in / people getting over it." That's also something in poetry's domain; reading and writing it help move us through sorrow and pain, and on to the other side. Poetry leads toward transformation. If you write and read, your compassion and understanding expand. Poetry can accompany us on our journeys. It makes one less alone.

In the end, it comes down to love, whether seen through the work of George Herbert, Derek Walcott, or Lucille Clifton, or through the actions of your very own life. These poems are to read—to grapple with, to question. Bring your complex nature to this work, the part of you that seeks revenge and the part of you that forgives.

—PATRICE VECCHIONE

"MY HEART, YOU MIGHT PIERCE IT AND TAKE IT"

My heart, you might pierce it and take it,
You take it, you pierce it, you take it,
You might pierce it and take it,
You my older brothers here,
You Bear here,
You Mountain Lion here,
You Wildcat here,
You my older brothers,
My heart, you might pierce it and take it.

SONG FROM A QUECHAN MYTH, "KUKUMAT BECAME SICK"

(Translated by Abraham Halpern)

ONLY CHERRIES?

They didn't want me around
Said I couldn't have no cherries
Or watch them pick cherries
Or even stand near the table
Where one of those Kultur-Kookie-Klucks
With the big fat-legged smile
Was fixing to pop a nice red cherry
In on top of his gold spoon
You know I don't like those people
Who act as if a cherry
Was something they'd personally thought up

KENNETH PATCHEN

DOGS

Five (was I?) when Edward Sanderlin, Ford Plant employee and nearby neighbor, flattened like gum the first mongrel bitch I ever loved. Uncle Carl home from the night shift, more than halfway to bed and dream, Edward not three minutes shy when he passed our hushed house and hit a bump that squealed. Slammed the brakes, spun the wheel, sent that Fairlane 500 death coach skidding for briars and bramble. In the mirror's frame, regardless: downed fur and splintered bones, the leaking blood of a dumb but loyal heart. Sleepy negligence? Simple bad luck? Even now I have no patience for such distinctions. On our gray, pocked steps the killer knocked and fidgeted in light too new for brilliance, florid-faced, aggrieved, forced to confess to a pitiless child. I swear I would have killed him if I could—him and his tortured face, asking for it (almost). "You didn't mean to do it, Edward, we know that," my mother assured, as his begging eyes sought mine and doubted. All morning long, curled in a wombish ball, I cried for my mutt's dead hide and liberated soul, lost companion for ditch digs, holly hunts, those low-spirited days when both weather and imagination failed me. Inconsolably sunk in the past, I had no inkling of what loomed ahead: a half dozen hounds, all destined for car fodder, trapper bait, distemper's foamy finish. Time and again I fell in love with a whimpering pup and with each lime-and-bedsheet burial lost faith in a miracle-working God. Of necessity a child learns to substitute what is for what was, grows up, moves on. Edward Sanderlin didn't ruin my life; he killed my dog, apologized, turned his back, walked away, drove home on gut-streaked tires and lived another 35 years: unindicted, unforgiven.

KAT MEADS

ENEMIES

If you are not to become a monster,
you must care what they think.
If you care what they think,

how will you not hate them,
and so become a monster
of the opposite kind? From where then

is love to come—love for your enemy
that is the way of liberty?
From forgiveness. Forgiven, they go

free of you, and you of them;
they are to you as sunlight
on a green branch. You must not

think of them again, except
as monsters like yourself,
pitiable because unforgiving.

WENDELL BERRY

SAY YOU LOVE ME

What happened earlier I'm not sure of.
Of course he was drunk, but often he was.
His face looked like a ham on a hook above

me—I was pinned to the chair because
he'd hunkered over me with arms like jaws
pried open by the chair arms. "Do you love

me?" he began to sob. "Say you love me!"
I held out. I was probably fifteen.
What had happened? Had my mother—had she

said or done something? Or had he just been
drinking too long after work? "He'll get *mean*,"
my sister hissed, "just *tell* him." I brought my knee

up to kick him, but was too scared. Nothing
could have got the words out of me then. Rage
shut me up, yet "DO YOU?" was beginning

to peel, as of live layers of skin, age
from age from age from him until he gazed
through hysteria as a wet baby thing

repeating, "Do you love me? Say you do,"
in baby chokes, only loud, for they came
from a man. There wouldn't be a rescue

from my mother, still at work. The same
choking sobs said, "Love me, love me," and my game
was breaking down because I couldn't do

anything, not escape into my own
refusal, *I won't, I won't,* not fantasize
a kind, rich father, not fill the narrowed zone,

empty except for confusion until the size
of my fear ballooned as I saw his eyes,
blurred, taurean—my sister screamed—unknown,

unknown to me, a voice rose and leveled
off, "I love you," I said. *"Say 'I love you,*
Dad!' " "I love you, Dad," I whispered, leveled

by defeat into a cardboard image, untrue,
unbending. I was surprised I could move
as I did to get up, but he stayed, burled

onto the chair—my monstrous fear—she screamed,
my sister, "Dad, the phone! Go answer it!"
The phone wasn't ringing, yet he seemed

to move toward it, and I ran. He had a fit—
"It's not ringing!"—but I was at the edge of it
as he collapsed into the chair and blamed

both of us at a distance. No, the phone
was not ringing. There was no world out there,
so there we remained, completely alone.

MOLLY PEACOCK

SUGARMOTHER'S DAUGHTER DREAMS

These are the same hands that stroke my head in fever.
But no. Her upper lip and teeth protrude over her chin.
An indentation runs from lip to cheekbones
as though she wore a metal bit in her mouth
when she was young, the bones still soft and forming.

She pushes my head back, pulls my hair, I watch the white
ceiling for pigeons to unfold and push her hands away.
But no birds become flesh and wing from plaster.
Holding a pink ten-pound bag, she pours sugar
down my throat so quickly I can't swallow,
my mouth filling like a leather jug,
the sugar overflowing. Her eyes spin out of focus
like a machine above my head. I choke
on the sweetness, the sugar falling on my shoulders
down the front of my blouse.

What horse are you mother, with the bit marks
on your face? What devil, yanking my head back so far?
If I could lift my hand to my forehead
I would make the sign of the cross, ask for forgiveness,
God, so that my real mother would return
in her blue dress and sandals.
But my arms are frozen at my sides, held down by her
grasping, by the sugar, the weight of the sugar
pouring down my black throat.

PATRICE VECCHIONE

FIRST MEMORY

Long ago, I was wounded. I lived
to revenge myself
against my father, not
for what he was—
for what I was: from the beginning of time,
in childhood, I thought
that pain meant
I was not loved.
It meant I loved.

LOUISE GLÜCK

REVENGE FABLE

There was a person
Could not get rid of his mother
As if he were her topmost twig.
So he pounded and hacked at her
With numbers and equations and laws
Which he invented and called truth.
He investigated, incriminated
And penalized her, like Tolstoy,
Forbidding, screaming and condemning,
Going for her with a knife,
Obliterating her with disgusts
Bulldozers and detergents
Requisitions and central heating
Rifles and whisky and bored sleep.

With all her babes in her arms, in ghostly weepings,
She died.

His head fell off like a leaf.

TED HUGHES

GRIEF

Grief reached across the world to get me,
sadness carries me across seas and countries
to your grave, my brother,

to offer the only gift I still can give you—
words you will not hear.

Fortune has taken you from me. You.
No reason, nothing fair.
I didn't deserve losing you.

Now, in the silence since,
as is the ancient custom of our people,
I say the mourner's prayer,
do the final kindness.

Accept and understand it, brother.
My head aches from crying.
Forever, goodbye.

GAIUS VALERIUS CATULLUS
(*Translated by Jacob Rabinowitz*)

MINE ENEMY IS GROWING OLD

Mine enemy is growing old,—
I have at last revenge.
The palate of the hate departs;
If any would avenge,—

Let him be quick, the viand flits,
It is a faded meat.
Anger as soon as fed is dead;
'Tis starving makes it fat.

EMILY DICKINSON

REVENGE

Mans disposition is for to requite
An injurie, before a benefite:
Thanksgiving is a burden, and a paine;
Revenge is pleasing to us, as our gaine.

ROBERT HERRICK

A CURSE ON A THIEF

Paul Dempster had a handsome tackle box
In which he'd stored up gems for many years:
Hooks marvelously sharp, ingenious lures
Jointed to look alive. He went to Fox

Lake, placed it on his dock, went in and poured
Himself a frosty Coors, returned to find
Some craven sneak had stolen in behind
His back and crooked his entire treasure hoard.

Bad cess upon the bastard! May the bass
He catches with Paul Dempster's pilfered gear
Jump from his creel, make haste for his bare rear,
And, fins outthrust, slide up his underpass.

May each ill-gotten catfish in his pan
Sizzle his lips and peel away the skin.
May every perch his pilfered lines reel in
Oblige him to spend decades on the can.

May he be made to munch a pickerel raw,
Its steely eyes fixed on him as he chews,
Choking on every bite, while metal screws
Inexorably lock his lower jaw,

And having eaten, may he be transformed
Into a trout himself, with gills and scales,

A stupid gasper that a hook impales.
In Hell's hot griddle may he be well warmed

And served with shots of lava-on-the-rocks
To shrieking imps indifferent to his moans
Who'll rend his skin and pick apart his bones,
Poor fish who hooked Paul Dempster's tackle box.

X. J. KENNEDY

"I WILL WRITE SONGS AGAINST YOU"

I will write songs against you,
enemies of my people; I will pelt you
with the winged seeds of the dandelion;
I will marshal against you
the fireflies of the dusk.

CHARLES REZNIKOFF

(*From* Separate Way)

A CURSE ON MINE-OWNERS

May God above
Send down a dove
With wings as sharp as razors
To cut the throats
Of those old bloats
Who cut poor miners' wages!

ANONYMOUS

SONNET XC

Then hate me when thou wilt, if ever, now,
Now, while the world is bent my deeds to cross,
Join with the spite of Fortune, make me bow,
And do not drop in for an after-loss.
Ah do not, when my heart hath 'scaped this sorrow,
Come in the rearward of a conquered woe;
Give not a windy night a rainy morrow
To linger out a purposed overthrow.
If thou wilt leave me, do not leave me last,
When other petty griefs have done their spite,
But in the onset come, so shall I taste
At first the very worst of Fortune's might,
    And other strains of woe, which now seem woe,
    Compared with loss of thee, will not seem so.

WILLIAM SHAKESPEARE

"ENVENOMED ARE MY SONGS"

Envenomed are my songs,
How could it be otherwise, tell?
Since you trickled poison
Into my life's clear well.

Envenomed are my songs,
How could it be otherwise, tell?
My heart holds many serpents,
And you, my love, as well.

HEINRICH HEINE

(Translated by Walter Arndt)

REVENGE

Revenge is a naked sword;
   It has neither hilt nor guard;
Wouldst thou wield this brand of the Lord?
   Is thy grasp, then, firm and hard?

But the closer thy clutch of the blade,
   The deadlier blow thou wouldst deal,
Deeper wound in thy hand is made—
   It is thy blood reddens the steel.

And when thou hast dealt the blow—
   When the blade from thy hand has flown—
Instead of the heart of the foe,
   Thou may'st find it sheathed in thine own.

CHARLES HENRY WEBB

BITTER FRUIT OF THE TREE

They said to my grandmother: "Please do not be bitter,"
When they sold her first-born and let the second die,
When they drove her husband till he took to the
    swamplands,
And brought him home bloody and beaten at last.
They told her, "It is better you should not be bitter,
Some must work and suffer so that we, who must,
    can live,
Forgiving is noble, you must not be heathen bitter:
These are your orders, you *are* not to be bitter."
And they left her shack for their porticoed house.

They said to my father: "Please do not be bitter."
When he ploughed and planted a crop not his,
When he weatherstripped a house that he could not
    enter,
And stored away a harvest he could not enjoy.
They answered his questions: "It does not concern you,
It is not for you to know, it is past your understanding,
All you need know is: you must not be bitter."
And they laughed on their way to reckon the crop,
And my father walked over the wide garnered acres
Where a cutting wind warned him of the cold to come.

They said to my brother: "Please do not be bitter,
Is it not sad to see the old place go to ruin?
The eaves are sprung and the chimney tower is leaning,

The sills, joists, and columns are rotten in the core;
The blinds hang crazy and the shingles blow away,
The fields have gone back to broomsedge and pine,
And the soil washes down the red gulley scars.
With so much to be done, there's no time for being bitter.
Your father made it for us, it is up to you to save it,
What is past is over, and you should not be bitter."
But my brother is bitter, and he does not hear.

STERLING A. BROWN

HYGIENE

*According to police officials, the 20-year-old suspect
and his girlfriend drove into a Shell service station on
Jan. 11 about 4:45 p.m. The restrooms were locked. The
suspect began to urinate in a planter box. The station
owner tapped the suspect on the leg and told him he
would get the restroom key. The man retaliated by pushing
the owner in the chest. Seeing his father fall, the owner's
son allegedly punched the suspect. The suspect fled and
reportedly returned to the station before 7 p.m., shooting
the station owner in the head.*

If the restroom door had been unlocked. If he had one
less beer. If the girlfriend hadn't been there to watch. If
there was something better on TV. If he had taken mass
transit instead. If he had to go number two. If we weren't
playing for laughs. If he didn't live across the street. If
I hadn't overheard his aunt ask him on Sunday, "What
are you going to do with your life?" and he hadn't
screamed, "I got ten bucks in my pocket and a car that
don't work." If I had said something. If his mother hadn't
tried heroin the first time. If he owned a Chevron card. If
the girlfriend was preggers. If I could comfort the son
who lost his father and the customers who had to wait.
If it had been raining. If he was modest. If I were a pacifist and you were a pacifist and he were a pacifist and
she were a pacifist. If there were no penalties, death or
otherwise. If the price of gas had fallen as a body

falls, without warning. If he had reached satori at 4:44 p.m., without warning. If the restroom door had been unlocked:

could we wash our hands of it?

TONI MIROSEVICH

ENVY

Malicious Envy rode
Upon a ravenous wolf, and still did chaw
Between his cankered teeth a venemous toad,
That all the poison ran about his chaw;[1]
But inwardly he chawèd his own maw[2]
At neighbours' wealth, that made him ever sad;
For death it was, when any good he saw,
And wept, that cause of weeping none he had,
But when he heard of harm, he wexèd wondrous glad.

All in a kirtle of discoloured say[3]
He clothèd was, ypainted full of eyes;
And in his bosom secretly there lay
An hateful snake, the which his tail upties
In many folds, and mortal sting implies.
Still as he rode, he gnashed his teeth to see
Those heaps of gold with griple[4] covetise,
And grudgèd at the great felicity
Of proud Lucifera, and his own company.

He hated all good works and virtuous deeds,
And him no less, that any like did use,
And who with gracious bread the hungry feeds,
His alms for want of faith he doth accuse;
So every good to bad he doth abuse:
And eke[5] the verse of famous poets' wit

He does backbite, and spiteful poison spews
From leprous mouth on all that ever writ:
Such one vile Envy was, that fifte in row did sit.

EDMUND SPENSER

(*From* The Faerie Queene, I, iv)

---

[1] *chaw: chops.*
[2] *maw: guts.*
[3] *kirtle of discoloured say: motley-colored woolen coat or tunic.*
[4] *griple: greedy.*
[5] *eke: also.*

A RITUAL TO READ TO EACH OTHER

If you don't know the kind of person I am
and I don't know the kind of person you are
a pattern that others made may prevail in the world
and following the wrong god home we may miss our star.

For there is many a small betrayal in the mind,
a shrug that lets the fragile sequence break
sending with shouts the horrible errors of childhood
storming out to play through the broken dyke.

And as elephants parade holding each elephant's tail,
but if one wanders the circus won't find the park,
I call it cruel and maybe the root of all cruelty
to know what occurs but not recognize the fact.

And so I appeal to a voice, to something shadowy,
a remote important region in all who talk:
though we could fool each other, we should consider—
lest the parade of our mutual life get lost in the dark.

For it is important that awake people be awake,
or a breaking line may discourage them back to sleep;
the signals we give—yes or no, or maybe—
should be clear: the darkness around us is deep.

WILLIAM STAFFORD

CATCH

My father came home with a new glove,
all tight stitches and unscuffed gold,
its deep pocket exhaling baseball,
signed by Mays, or Mantle, or The Man,
or some lesser god I've since forgotten.
He took off his tie and dark jacket
and we went outside to break it in,
throwing the ball back and forth
in the dusk, the big man sweating
already, grunting as he tried
to fire it at his son, who saw now,
for the first time, that his father
who loved to talk baseball at dinner
and let him stay up late to watch the fights
unfold like grainy nightmares
on Gillette's Cavalcade of Sports,
the massive father, who could lift him
high in the air with one hand,
threw like a girl—far and away
the worst we could say of anyone—
his off-kilter windup and release
like a raw confession, so naked
and helpless in the failing light
that thirty years later, still
feeling the ball's soft kiss in my glove,
I'm afraid to throw it back.

GEORGE BILGERE

SEA OF FAITH

Once when I was teaching "Dover Beach"
to a class of freshmen, a young woman
raised her hand and said, "I'm confused
about this 'Sea of Faith.' " "Well," I said,
"let's talk about it. We probably need
to talk a bit about figurative language.
What confuses you about it?"
"I mean, is it a real sea?" she asked.
"You mean, is it a real body of water
that you could point to on a map
or visit on a vacation?"
"Yes," she said. "Is it a *real* sea?"
Oh Christ, I thought, is this where we are?
Next year I'll be teaching them the alphabet
and how to sound words out.
I'll have to teach them geography, apparently,
before we can move on to poetry.
I'll have to teach them history, too—
a few weeks on the Dark Ages might be instructive.
"Yes," I wanted to say, "it is.
It is a real sea. In fact it flows
right into the Sea of Ignorance
IN WHICH YOU ARE DROWNING.
Let me throw you a Rope of Salvation
before the Sharks of Desire gobble you up.
Let me hoist you back up onto this Ship of Fools
so that we might continue our search
for the Fountain of Youth. Here, take a drink

of this. It's fresh from the River of Forgetfulness."
But of course I didn't say any of that.
I tried to explain in such a way
as to protect her from humiliation,
tried to explain that poets
often speak of things that don't exist.
It was only much later that I wished
I could have answered differently,
only after I'd betrayed myself
and been betrayed that I wished
it was true, wished there really was a Sea of Faith
that you could wade out into,
dive under its blue and magic waters,
hold your breath, swim like a fish
down to the bottom, and then emerge again
able to believe in everything, faithful
and unafraid to ask even the simplest of questions,
happy to have them simply answered.

JOHN BREHM

TO A BAD HEART

Speak, thou jaded heart, defective heart,
heart kneaded with cold water, scraggy heart,
short-winded heart, devourous heart, hooked heart,
ass-ridden, over-lechered, plucked-up heart,
bestunk, maleficated, lumpish, prolix
heart, heart, heart, beblistered, seedless, void:
What will you promise now? Last time you swore—
remember? in the barn?—things would be different;
but nothing's ever different. And I'm fed up.
Get out! This time I swear I'm serious. Heart,
I've longed to see you dead. I've dreamed of you
cold as a cow's heart in a butcher's showcase
jutting your battleship big guns, a beef-chunk
blood-drained, koshered, pure. I tell you, heart,
you World's Most Perfectly Developed Heart,
bottlecap-bender unable to touch your ear,
armpit-razored oiled bronze bulging hulk,
those flabby fairy hearts that whistle at you
are such as kick chairs in their scrawny rage,
frustrated, pimply, adolescent hearts
who know you only on the comic covers
posed like a rock of muscle. Oh, I have seen you,
heart, yes you, you Cardiac Giant, cringe
before a simple heart one-half your size,
solaced you dragging your bruised auricles home,
aorta between your legs like a booted dog,
snivelling of some gang of bullies. Sero
te amavi, tough but O so gentle.

Compare those swollen ventricles with the hard
lissome chambers of any healthy heart,
grown through those flexions natural to hearts
tough and able to take care of itself,
not bloated like a vacuum cleaner bag
with strained, incessant, unnatural exercise.
You ought to be ashamed, you hear me, heart?
What did I do to deserve a heart like you?

TIM REYNOLDS

BLINK

I was small and half-believed I could disappear
just by closing my eyes—no,
I wished for it fervently:
that my scarred hands, red with itch,
would become the ghostly hands of saints;
the dark oval of my face dissolve,
transparent as the air.
How does a child fit a body she hates?
How does a child learn to hate what she is?
At school I was *wool-locks, chink-eyes, freak;*
each slur spat—a twisted
animal, some trapped thing thrown back, maimed.
In church, the gravest of my sins
in the hushed confessional: *this flesh,*
which, bead by bead, I prayed might be illumined,
    changed, erased.

Oh, I would have died to be beautiful once
—*Saint Cecilia, Saint Genevieve*—
wrapped myself in the scratchy sheets
to be buried, and risen again;
to blink and vanish—look:
here's how the world turns a girl on the wheel of herself,
what wasn't murdered in me:
a face that stares back from the glass of its longed-for
    death,
alive, and loves what it sees.

CECILIA WOLOCH

STRONGER LESSONS

Have you learn'd lessons only of those who admired you,
    and were tender with you, and stood aside for you?
Have you not learn'd great lessons from those who reject
    you, and brace themselves against you? or who treat
    you with contempt, or dispute the passage with you?

WALT WHITMAN

A PACT

I make a pact with you, Walt Whitman—
I have detested you long enough.
I come to you as a grown child
Who has had a pig-headed father;
I am old enough now to make friends.
It was you that broke the new wood,
Now is a time for carving.
We have one sap and one root—
Let there be commerce between us.

EZRA POUND

POEM

I lived in the first century of world wars.
Most mornings I would be more or less insane,
The newspapers would arrive with their careless stories,
The news would pour out of various devices
Interrupted by attempts to sell products to the unseen.
I would call my friends on other devices;
They would be more or less mad for similar reasons.
Slowly I would get to pen and paper,
Make my poems for others unseen and unborn.
In the day I would be reminded of those men and women
Brave, setting up signals across vast distances,
Considering a nameless way of living, of almost
    unimagined values.
As the lights darkened, as the lights of night brightened,
We would try to imagine them, try to find each other.
To construct peace, to make love, to reconcile
Waking with sleeping, ourselves with each other,
Ourselves with ourselves. We would try by any means
To reach the limits of ourselves, to reach beyond
    ourselves,
To let go the means, to wake.

I lived in the first century of these wars.

MURIEL RUKEYSER

TO A TERRORIST

For the historical ache, the ache passed down
which finds its circumstance and becomes
the present ache, I offer this poem

without hope, knowing there's nothing,
not even revenge, which alleviates
a life like yours. I offer it as one

might offer his father's ashes
to the wind, a gesture
when there's nothing else to do.

Still, I must say to you:
I hate your good reasons.
I hate the hatefulness that makes you fall

in love with death, your own included.
Perhaps you're hating me now,
I who own my own house

and live in a country so muscular,
so smug, it thinks its terror is meant
only to mean well, and to protect.

Christ turned his singular cheek,
one man's holiness another's absurdity.
Like you, the rest of us obey the sting,

the surge. I'm just speaking out loud
to cancel my silence. Consider it an old impulse,
doomed to become mere words.

The first poet probably spoke to thunder
and, for a while, believed
thunder had an ear and a choice.

STEPHEN DUNN

THE MINEFIELD

He was running with his friend from town to town.
They were somewhere between Prague and Dresden.
He was fourteen. His friend was faster
and knew a shortcut through the fields they could take.
He said there was lettuce growing in one of them,
and they hadn't eaten all day. His friend ran a few lengths
    ahead,
like a wild rabbit across the grass,
turned his head, looked back once,
and his body was scattered across the field.

My father told us this, one night,
and then continued eating dinner.

He brought them with him—the minefields.
He carried them underneath his good intentions.
He gave them to us—in the volume of his anger,
in the bruises we covered up with sleeves.
In the way he threw anything against the wall—
a radio, that wasn't even ours,
a melon, once, opened like a head.
In the way we still expect, years later and continents away,
that anything might explode at any time,
and we would have to run on alone
with a vision like that
only seconds behind.

DIANE THIEL

WHAT THEY WANTED

was my soul, my body, my mind.
Instead what they got
was a declaration
to wage war on the war.

In the Nam,
during my relationship
between the manipulated
and the manipulator,
I was nothing more
than U.S. Grade A American meat
used for some bureaucrat's political gain.

Now over thirty years later
in this war of no fronts,
an MIA in my own country,
I sleep lightly,
keep a knife nearby on the night stand,
continue to go on night patrols,
look for an alternative revenge.

VICTOR H. BAUSCH

Milton, the airport driver, retired now
from trucking, who ferried me
from the Greenville-Spartanburg airport
to Athens last Sunday midnight to 2:30 A.M.,
tells me about his son, Tom, just back
from the Gulf war. "He's at Fort Stewart
with the 102nd Mechanized, the first tank unit
over the line, not a shot fired at them.
His job was to check the Iraqi tanks
that the airstrikes hit, hundreds of them.
The boy had never even come up on a car accident
here at home, twenty-four years old. Can you
imagine what he lifted the lid to find?
Three helmets with heads in them staring
from the floor, and that's just one tank.
He has screaming flashbacks, can't talk about it
anymore. I just told him to be strong
and put it out of his mind. With time,
if you stay strong, those things'll go away.
Or they'd find a bunker, one of those holes
they hid in, and yell something in American,
and wait a minute, and then roll grenades in
and check it and find nineteen freshly killed guys,
some sixty, some fourteen, real thin.
They were just too scared to move.
He feels pretty bad about it, truthfully,
all this yellow ribbon celebrating.
It wasn't a war really. I mean, he says

it was just piles and piles of their bodies.
Some of his friends got sick, started vomiting,
and had to be walked back to the rear.
Looks like to me it could have been worked
some other way. My boy came through OK,
but he won't go back, I'll tell you that.
He's getting out as soon as he can.
First chance comes, he'll be in Greenville
selling cars, or fixing them. He's good at both.
Pretty good carpenter too. You know how I know?
He'll tear the whole thing out if it's not right
and start over. There's some that'll look
at a board that's not flush and say *shit,
nail it,* but he can't do that, Tom."

COLEMAN BARKS

HERO

He's a hero, says the soldier in fatigues, pointing at the kid kneeling on the parquet floor. Killed a Chetnik, he says. The boy put the ammunition belt and the old M48 down on the floor: he smiles, completely carried away, as he plays with plastic cars and makes the sounds of an engine. On Vraca, he says, after agreeing to tell the story, my friends took some shots with a kalashnikov and nothing. Then I let go twice and the Chetnik just rolled over. My rifle kills at ten miles, he said, scratching his forehead with a toy car.

SEMEZDIN MEHMEDINOVIC

(Translated by Ammiel Alcalay)

FROM HENRY V, *ACT IV, SCENE I*

But if the cause be not good, the King himself hath a heavy reckoning to make, when all those legs and arms and heads, chopp'd off in a battle, shall join together at the latter day and cry all, "We died at such a place"— some swearing, some crying for a surgeon, some upon their wives left poor behind them, some upon the debts they owe, some upon their children rawly left. I am afeard there are few die well that die in a battle; for how can they charitably dispose of any thing, when blood is their argument? Now, if these men do not die well, it will be a black matter for the King that led them to it.

WILLIAM SHAKESPEARE

Do you have any scissors I could borrow? *No, I'm sorry I
don't.* What about a knife? You got any knives? A good par-
ing knife would do or a simple butcher knife or maybe a
cleaver? *No, sorry all I have is this old bread knife my
grandfather used to butter his bread with every morning.*
Well then, how about a hand drill or hammer, a bike
chain, or some barbed wire? You got any rusty razor-edged
barbed wire? You got a chain saw? *No, sorry I don't.* Well
then maybe you might have some sticks? *I'm sorry I don't
have any sticks.* How about some stones? *No, I don't have
any sticks or stones.* Well how about a stone tied to a stick?
You mean a club? Yeah, a club. You got a club? *No, sorry, I
don't have any clubs.* What about some fighting picks, war
axes, military forks, or tomahawks? *No, sorry, I don't have
any kind of war fork, axe, or tomahawk.* What about a
morning star? *A morning star?* Yeah, you know, those
spiked ball and chains they sell for riot control. *No, nothing like that. Sorry.* Now, I know you said you don't have a
knife except for that dull old thing your grandfather used
to butter his bread with every morning and he passed
down to you but I thought maybe you just might have an
Australian dagger with a quartz blade and a wood handle,
or a bone dagger, or a Bowie, you know it doesn't hurt to
ask? Or perhaps one of those lethal multipurpose stilet-
tos? *No, sorry.* Or maybe you have a simple blow pipe? Or
a complex airgun? *No, I don't have a simple blow pipe or
a complex airgun.* Well then maybe you have a jungle
carbine, a Colt, a revolver, a Ruger, an axis bolt-action

repeating rifle with telescopic sight for sniping, a sawed-off shotgun? Or better yet, a gas-operated self-loading fully automatic assault weapon? *No, sorry I don't.* How about a hand grenade? *No.* How about a tank? *No.* Shrapnel? *No.* Napalm? *No.* Napalm 2. *No, sorry I don't.* Let me ask you this. Do you have any intercontinental ballistic missiles? Or submarine-launched cruise missiles? Or multiple independently targeted reentry missiles? Or terminally guided anti-tank shells or projectiles? Let me ask you this. Do you have any fission bombs or hydrogen bombs? Do you have any thermonuclear warheads? Got any electronic measures or electronic counter-measures or electronic counter-counter-measures? Got any biological weapons or germ warfare, preferably in aerosol form? Got any enhanced tactical neutron lasers emitting massive doses of whole-body gamma radiation? Wait a minute. Got any plutonium? Got any chemical agents, nerve agents, blister agents, you know, like mustard gas, any choking agents or incapacitating agents or toxin agents? *Well I'm not sure. What do they look like?* Liquid vapor powder colorless gas. Invisible. *I'm not sure. What do they smell like?* They smell like fruit, garlic, fish or soap, new-mown hay, apple blossoms, or like those little green peppers that your grandfather probably would tend to in his garden every morning after he buttered his bread with that old bread knife that he passed down to you.

CATHERINE BOWMAN

ANOTHER VIGIL AT SAN QUENTIN

Not quite midnight. My candle stutters
under the half-full moon, the frightened stars.

Someday in the future, people will be curious
about these rituals: how
we murdered them at dead of night, strapped to beds,
poison injections dripping, scientifically timed,
thinking ourselves modern.

And some of us, guards,
(two rows of them here, visors
pushed back, batons at the ready),
and some, newsmen, clambering over low rooftops
with their kleig lights and cameras.
And the rest of us drabs, like weary and defiant protesters,
arm in arm, with our candles and sage

and We Shall Overcome and in this case eagle feathers,
as the accused killer
(all right, he really did it)
is a Native American, who
(if you want the whole story)
lured a girl-child to his car,
raped her—go on tell it—stripped and flung
this ten-year-old from a bridge
into a gully, as if she were a beer can he'd just crushed
under his heel, and left for litter.

Say that part. And then, to enact
our rage, express our unspeakable
horror at the ravage of our daughter,
we'll carefully poison him.
The candles burn down.
The counter-protesters get on their megaphone.
"Ten minutes to repent! Nine more minutes
or your soul will burn!
Eight minutes and the Lord is your judge!"

Our songs pick up as well; We Shall Not
We Shall Not Be Moved,
Gonna Lay Down My Sword and Shield,
and a Navajo chant.
The current swells. Inside,
a frightened, messed-up
man is being prepared for death and burial.
He has requested that a medicine man, with sage,
accompany him in his death chamber. Request denied.

All right, one eagle feather,
to be pinned to the sheet over his body.
I link arms with the rough wool coat
next to me, bow my head into a friend's shoulder,
thinking about my own rape
at the hands of a rageful drunk, years ago.

I don't have words
for what I'm doing here, only the smell

of the ocean going on and on below us,
crash, smash, gotcha.
And the softness of the air on my cheeks,
and the sound of screaming gulls.
Last week the rains finally stopped.
The peach tree is in full pink flower.
Earth seems to have forgiven
our uncountable human sins again
and opened her arms to us in Spring. O pure

right and wrong, how I long for you.
Tell the people of the future I came here
for confusion and ignorance and darkness.
For for the smell of candle wax
dripping silently and slowly,
the white lick of flame against the char of ash.
For poison and reason and the old moon,
and a stubborn idea about the innocence of things.

ALISON LUTERMAN

PRAYER

I want a god
as my accomplice
who spends nights
in houses
of ill repute
and gets up late
on Saturdays

a god
who whistles
through the streets
and trembles
before the lips
of his lover

a god
who waits in line
at the entrance
of movie houses
and likes to drink
café au lait

a god
who spits
blood from
tuberculosis and
doesn't even have
enough for bus fare

a god
knocked
unconscious
by the billy club
of a policeman
at a demonstration

a god
who pisses
out of fear
before the flaring
electrodes
of torture

a god
who hurts
to the last
bone and
bites the air
in pain

a jobless god
a striking god
a hungry god
a fugitive god
an exiled god
an enraged god

a god
who longs

from jail
for a change
in the order
of things

I want a
more godlike
god

FRANCISCO X. ALARCÓN

WHY PEOPLE MURDER

I found out why people murder
in the kitchen of our house in Boulder Creek
where we'd made soybean patties,
dozens of soybean patties
ground up in our Vitamix blender and stacked,
in Saran Wrap, in the freezer.

He was in the living room.
In navy blue sweat pants and sheepskin slippers
and his pipe—he was tamping tobacco
with his thumb and looking for matches.

I picked up the knife we'd used to chop onions—
onions and carrots and whatever else it was
we put in those hopeful dry little cakes.

The details of this particular fight
are lost. But trust me, they don't matter.
Just imagine need, primitive, a baby screaming
for the tit; lust, the clawing
into another, wanting to part the other like water,
and be taken in.

And desperation, that's the big one.
You're shaky as a junkie, the pain
hums, an electric current.
You're frozen to it, a dog who's
gnawed on a cord and must be kicked off.

Save me. I'm frantic. I'm on my knees, prostrate.
I'm flat as wax across the linoleum floor.

The knife is clean. I washed it after the onions.
I lurch into the living room. My breath
comes out visible, like in cold weather.
When he sees me, he's startled, doesn't
know if he should be scared.
I'm emanating like a rod of uranium.
He says my name, tentative. I look down
at the knife, as if I were carrying it to the drawer
and took a wrong turn.

ELLEN BASS

KISSIE LEE

Toughest gal I ever did see
Was a gal by the name of Kissie Lee;
The toughest gal God ever made
And she drew a dirty, wicked blade.

Now this here gal warn't always tough
Nobody dreamed she'd turn out rough
But her Grammaw Mamie had the name
Of being the town's sin and shame.

When Kissie Lee was young and good
Didn't nobody treat her like they should
Allus gettin' beat by a no-good shine
An' allus quick to cry and whine.

Till her Grammaw said, "Now listen to me,
I'm tiahed of yoah whinin', Kissie Lee.
People don't ever treat you right,
An' you allus scrappin' or in a fight."

"Whin I was a gal wasn't no soul
Could do me wrong an' still stay whole.
Ah got me a razor to talk for me
An' aftah that they let me be."

Well Kissie Lee took her advice
And after that she didn't speak twice

'Cause when she learned to stab and run
She got herself a little gun.

And from that time that gal was mean,
Meanest mama you ever seen.
She could hold her likker and hold her man
And she went thoo life jus' raisin' san'.

One night she walked in Jim's saloon
And seen a guy what spoke too soon;
He done her dirt long time ago
When she was good and feeling low.

Kissie bought her drink and she paid her dime
Watchin' this guy what beat her time
And he was making for the outside door
When Kissie shot him to the floor.

Not a word she spoke but she switched her blade
And flashing that lil ole baby paid:
Evvy livin' guy got out of her way
Because Kissie Lee was drawin' her pay.

She could shoot glass offa the hinges,
She could take herself on the wildest binges.
And she died with her boots on switching blades
On Talladega Mountain in the likker raids.

MARGARET WALKER

POISON

Curly had once seen arrows poisoned,
the rattler pinned with a forked stick,
tickled the length of its body, angered,
a deer liver dangled before it, the rattler
striking the liver, sinking fangs into it
three, four, five times, then pinned again,
furious, unpinned to strike the liver again
that blackened & emitted a sour smell.
Arrows were thrust into it, withdrawn,
dried in the sun, a glistening scum adhering,
which, if it touched raw flesh, meant death.
Now, Crazy Horse would stuff that liver,
entire, into the white man's mouth.

WILLIAM HEYEN

"LOVE BADE ME WELCOME: YET MY SOUL DREW BACK"

Love bade me welcome: yet my soul drew back,
      Guilty of dust and sin.
But quick-eyed Love, observing me grow slack
      From my first entrance in,
Drew nearer to me, sweetly questioning
      If I lacked anything.

"A guest," I answered, "worthy to be here":
      Love said, "You shall be he."
"I, the unkind, ungrateful? Ah, my dear,
      I cannot look on thee."
Love took my hand, and smiling did reply,
      "Who made the eyes but I?"

"Truth, Lord; but I have marred them; let my shame
      Go where it doth deserve."
"And know you not," says Love, "who bore the blame?"
      "My dear, then I will serve."
"You must sit down," says Love, "and taste my meat."
      So I did sit and eat.

GEORGE HERBERT

ELECTROCUTING AN ELEPHANT

Her handlers, dressed in vests and flannel pants,
    Step forward in the weak winter light
Leading a behemoth among elephants,
Topsy, to another exhibition site;
    Caparisoned with leather bridle,
Six impassive tons of carnival delight
Shambles on among spectators who sidle
    Nervously off, for the brute has killed
At least three men, most recently an idle
Hanger-on at shows, who, given to distilled
    Diversions, fed her a live cigar.
Since become a beast of burden, Topsy thrilled
The crowds in her palmy days, and soon will star
    Once more, in an electrocution,
Which incident, though it someday seem bizarre,
Is now a new idea in execution.

Topsy has been fed an unaccustomed treat,
    A few carrots laced with cyanide,
And copper plates have been fastened to her feet,
Wired to cables running off on either side:
    She stamps two times in irritation,
Then waits, for elephants, having a thick hide,
Know how to be patient. The situation
    Seems dreamlike, till someone throws a switch,
And the huge body shakes for the duration
Of five or six unending seconds, in which
    Smoke rises and Topsy's trunk contracts

And twelve thousand mammoth pounds finally pitch
To earth, as the current breaks and all relax.
   It is a scene shot with shades of grey—
The smoke, the animal, the reported facts—
On a seasonably grey and gloomy day.

Would you care to see any of that again?
   See it as many times as you please,
For an electrician, Thomas Edison,
Has had a bright idea we call the movies,
   And called on for monitory spark,
Has preserved it all in framed transparencies
That are clear as day, for all the day is dark.
   You might be amused on second glance
To note the background—it's an amusement park!—
A site on Coney Island where elephants
   Are being used in the construction,
And where Topsy, through a keeper's negligence,
Got loose, causing some property destruction,
   And so is shown to posterity,
A study in images and conduction,
Sunday, January 4th, 1903.

GEORGE BRADLEY

MALEDICTION

You who dump the beer cans in the lake;
Who in the strict woods sow
The bulbous polyethylene retorts;
Who from your farting car
With spiffy rear-suspension toss
Your tissues, mustard-streaked, upon
The generating moss; who drop
The squamules of your reckless play,
Grease-wrappers, unspare parts, lie-labeled
Cultures even flies would scorn
To spawn on—total Zed, my kinsman
Ass-on-wheels, my blare-bred bray
And burden,
                    may the nice crabs thread
Your private wilds with turnpikes; weasels'
Condoms squish between your toes,
And plastic-coated toads squat *plop*
Upon your morning egg—may gars
Come nudge you from your inner-tube,
Perch hiss you to the bottom, junked,
A discard, your dense self your last
Enormity.

BARRY SPACKS

THE APPARITION

When by thy scorne, O murdresse I am dead,
    And that thou thinkst thee free
From all solicitation from mee,
Then shall my ghost come to thy bed,
And thee, feigned vestall, in worse armes shall see;
Then thy sicke taper will begin to winke,
And he, whose thou art then, being tyr'd before,
Will, if thou stirre, or pinch to wake him, thinke
    Thou call'st for more,
And in false sleepe will from thee shrinke,
And then poore Aspen wretch, neglected thou
Bath'd in a cold quicksilver sweat wilt lye
    A veryer ghost than I;
What I will say, I will not tell thee now,
Lest that preserve thee; and since my love is spent,
I had rather thou shouldst painfully repent,
Than by my threatenings rest still innocent.

JOHN DONNE

NOTE FROM A LOVING WIFE

The dishes all want to break,
my love,
one by one
they wriggle
from my hands
shattering
in unsorry pieces

"Leave him," cries
the cracked bowl
"You are too much,"
whispers a shard of plate
"Too good," jagged mouth
of glass, "to be—here"

your very own dishes,
my love, betrayed you
spoons beat your secrets
'til they bent in fatigue

so when you come home
with her scent in your hair
and you walk from room
to room finding no sign
of me
keep your shoes on

particularly in the kitchen
as my freedom might get
stuck in your feet.

MARIAHADESSA EKERE TALLIE

"I HAD NEVER SEEN HER SO ANGRY"

I had never seen her so angry, and her rage revealed a measure of love I had missed. There were many times she might have hurt me that way, and didn't.

GARY YOUNG

WHEELS

He was a trafficker in hearts
Raced mine to 8,000 RPM
until we finally engaged

For that fast roaring time
it was the two of us taking turns
at 75 miles an hour
blasting the all-night stations
parking with the moon roof open

When his fuel pump froze up
he pulled the emergency brake
skidded onto the shoulder and waved me on
I spun out bad on the off ramp

Later,
passing his Ford in the lot
I fingered car keys
Pictured long silver wounds
scraped in the new black paint
Thought how it would be
to nick his whitewalls
just to give that shiny pickup
one last putdown.

SARAH RABKIN

ANY LOVER TO ANY BELOVED

Today, if the breath of breeze
wants to scatter petals in the garden of memory,
why shouldn't it?
                    If a forgotten pain
in some corner of the past
wants to burst into flame again, let it happen.
Though you act like a stranger now—
come—be close to me for a few minutes.
Though after this meeting
            we will know even better what we have lost,
and the gauze of words left unspoken
hangs between one line and another,
neither of us will mention our promises.
Nothing will be said of loyalty or faithlessness.

If my eyelashes want to tell you something
about wiping out the lines
left by the dust of time on your face,
you can listen or not, just as you like.
And what your eyes fail to hide from me—
            if you care to, of course you may say it,
            or not, as the case may be.

FAIZ AHMED FAIZ

(*Translated by Naomi Lazard*)

YOU CALLED ME *CORAZÓN*

That was enough
for me to forgive you.
To spirit a tiger
from its cell.

Called me *corazón*
in that instant before
I let go the phone
back to its cradle.

Your voice small.
Heat of your eyes,
how I would've placed
my mouth on each.

Said *corazón*
and the word blazed
like a branch of *jacaranda*.

SANDRA CISNEROS

QUATRAIN: FORGIVE ME NOT

Forgive me not! Hate me and I shall know
Some of Love's fire still burns within your breast!
Forgiveness finds its home in hearts at rest,
On dead volcanoes only lies the snow.

LILLA CABOT PERRY

JERUSALEM

Let's be the same wound if we must bleed.
Let's fight side by side, even if the enemy
is ourselves: I am yours, you are mine.
　　　—Tommy Olofsson, Sweden

I'm not interested in
who suffered the most.
I'm interested in
people getting over it.

Once when my father was a boy
a stone hit him on the head.
Hair would never grow there.
Our fingers found the tender spot
and its riddle: the boy who has fallen
stands up. A bucket of pears
in his mother's doorway welcomes him home.
The pears are not crying.
Later his friend who threw the stone
says he was aiming at a bird.
And my father starts growing wings.

Each carries a tender spot:
something our lives forgot to give us.
A man builds a house and says,
"I am native now."
A woman speaks to a tree in place
of her son. And olives come.

A child's poem says,
"I don't like wars,
they end up with monuments."
He's painting a bird with wings
wide enough to cover two roofs at once.

Why are we so monumentally slow?
Soldiers stalk a pharmacy:
big guns, little pills.
If you tilt your head just slightly
it's ridiculous.

There's a place in my brain
where hate won't grow.
I touch its riddle: wind, and seeds.
Something pokes us as we sleep.

It's late but everything comes next.

NAOMI SHIHAB NYE

FORGIVENESS

I heard the man
before I saw him.
He was kneeling
in an alley
off Broadway
and 45th street
one summer night,
rocking back and
forth, muttering,
"Forgive me!
Forgive me!"
At first, I thought
he was bending
over a dog, then
I thought, no, his grief
is too great: it
must be a child,
and I hurried to help.
There was no dog,
no child. The man
was bending
over his shadow,
pleading with it,
"Forgive me!
Forgive me!"

MORTON MARCUS

THE JEWISH TIME BOMB

On my desk is a stone with "Amen" carved on it, one
    survivor fragment
of the thousands upon thousands of bits of broken
    tombstones
in Jewish graveyards. I know all these broken pieces
now fill the great Jewish time bomb
along with the other fragments and shrapnel, broken
    Tablets of the Law
broken altars broken crosses rusty crucifixion nails
broken houseware and holyware and broken bones
eyeglasses shoes prostheses false teeth
empty cans of lethal poison. All these broken pieces
fill the Jewish time bomb until the end of days.
And though I know about all this, and about the end of
    days,
the stone on my desk gives me peace.
It is the touchstone no one touches, more philosophical
than any philosopher's stone, broken stone from a broken
    tomb
more whole than any wholeness,
a stone of witness to what has always been
and what will always be, a stone of amen and love.
Amen, amen, and may it come to pass.

YEHUDA AMICHAI
(*Translated by Chana Bloch and Chana Kronfeld*)

MENDING WALL

Something there is that doesn't love a wall
That sends the frozen-ground-swell under it,
And spills the upper boulders in the sun;
And makes gaps even two can pass abreast.
The work of hunters is another thing:
I have come after them and made repair
Where they have left not one stone on a stone,
But they would have the rabbit out of hiding,
To please the yelping dogs. The gaps I mean,
No one has seen them made or heard them made,
But at spring mending-time we find them there.
I let my neighbor know beyond the hill;
And on a day we meet to walk the line
And set the wall between us once again.
We keep the wall between us as we go.
To each the boulders that have fallen to each.
And some are loaves and some so nearly balls
We have to use a spell to make them balance:
"Stay where you are until our backs are turned!"
We wear our fingers rough with handling them.
Oh, just another kind of outdoor game,
One on a side. It comes to little more:
There where it is we do not need the wall:
He is all pine and I am apple orchard.
My apple trees will never get across
And eat the cones under his pines, I tell him.
He only says, "Good fences make good neighbors."
Spring is the mischief in me, and I wonder

If I could put a notion in his head:
"*Why* do they make good neighbors? Isn't it
Where there are cows? But here there are no cows.
Before I built a wall I'd ask to know
What I was walling in or walling out,
And to whom I was like to give offense.
Something there is that doesn't love a wall,
That wants it down." I could say "Elves" to him,
But it's not elves exactly, and I'd rather
He said it for himself. I see him there
Bringing a stone grasped firmly by the top
In each hand, like an old-stone savage armed.
He moves in darkness as it seems to me,
Not of woods only and the shade of trees.
He will not go behind his father's saying,
And he likes having thought of it so well
He says again, "Good fences make good neighbors."

ROBERT FROST

SONNET XXXV

No more be grieved at that which thou hast done:
Roses have thorns, and silver fountains mud,
Clouds and eclipses stain both moon and sun,
And loathsome canker lives in sweetest bud.
All men make faults, and even I in this,
Authorizing thy trespass with compare,
Myself corrupting salving thy amiss,
Excusing thy sins more than thy sins are:
For to thy sensual fault I bring in sense—
Thy adverse party is thy advocate—
And 'gainst myself a lawful plea commence:
Such civil war is in my love and hate
    That I an accessary needs must be
      To that sweet thief which sourly robs from me.

WILLIAM SHAKESPEARE

LOVE AFTER LOVE

The time will come
when, with elation,
you will greet yourself arriving
at your own door, in your own mirror,
and each will smile at the other's welcome,

and say, sit here. Eat.
You will love again the stranger who was your self.
Give wine. Give bread. Give back your heart
to itself, to the stranger who has loved you

all your life, whom you ignored
for another, who knows you by heart.
Take down the love letters from the bookshelf,

the photographs, the desperate notes,
peel your own image from the mirror.
Sit. Feast on your life.

DEREK WALCOTT

LET THERE BE NEW FLOWERING

let there be new flowering
in the fields let the fields
turn mellow for the men
let the men keep tender
through the time let the time
be wrested from the war
let the war be won
let love be
at the end

LUCILLE CLIFTON

BIOGRAPHICAL NOTES

The quotes contained within the biographies below are from interviews, letters, or readily available sources, such as those on the Internet.

FRANCISCO X. ALARCÓN (b. 1954), Chicano poet and educator, spent his first six years in California, then his family moved to Mexico. When he was eighteen he returned to California, and he's lived there since. Alarcón received his graduate degree from Stanford University. He is the author of ten books of poems, most recently *From the Other Side of Night / Del otro lado de la noche: New and Selected Poems.* He's also written several bilingual books for children. Alarcón is the recipient of Danforth and Fulbright fellowships and has been awarded several literary prizes, including the Before Columbus Foundation American Book Award, the PEN Oakland Josephine Miles Award, and the Fred Cody Lifetime Achievement Award by the Bay Area Book Reviewers Association. Alarcón currently teaches at the University of California, Davis.

Alarcón writes, "I read my poem 'Prayer' as part of the celebrations when my brother was ordained as a priest in the Holy Family Catholic Church in Wilmington, California. This church is located in the middle of a Latino barrio and my family was very involved in setting it up in the early 1920s because my great-grandmother and grandparents wanted a church that truly met the spiritual needs of the Mexican immigrants of that area. I read 'Prayer' in both English and Spanish, and my mother, present in the audience, almost fainted because of the way God is described in the poem. My brother Carlos, the recently ordained priest, was more understanding, and told me later that day that he found the poem moving and 'Christian,' since Christ had really experienced great human suffering for our redemption. My poem reflects the universal longing for a more just and humane world."

SELECTED READING

From the Other Side of Night / Del otro lado de la noche: New and Selected Poems (University of Arizona Press)

Sonnets to Madness and Other Misfortunes / Sonetos a la locura y otras penas (Creative Arts Books)

YEHUDA AMICHAI (1924–2000) was born in Germany, and in 1936 he immigrated with his family to Palestine when profound anti-Semitism made life in Germany extremely difficult for Jews. He became a naturalized Israeli citizen, lived in Jerusalem, and had great love for his adopted home. Amichai served in the Jewish Brigade of the British Army in World War II and fought with the Israeli defense forces in the 1948 Arab-Israeli war. Following the war, he attended Hebrew University and then taught school. Amichai, whose writing has been translated into thirty-seven languages, was the author of many books of poems, two novels, and a book of short stories. He received the Israel Prize for Poetry and was a foreign honorary member of the American Academy of Arts and Letters. On the day of Amichai's death, many Israeli radio stations aired readings of his poems, and people traveling on the buses that day in Jerusalem recited

Amichai's words along with the radio. His poetry is known by heart by many Israelis. Amichai was considered the poet patriarch of Israel; his verse, "the bread and water of poetry."

SELECTED READING

Open Closed Open: Poems (Chana Bloch and Chana Kronfeld, translators; Harcourt)

The Selected Poetry of Yehuda Amichai (Chana Bloch and Stephen Mitchell, translators; University of California Press)

ANONYMOUS ("A Curse on Mine-Owners") is an American folk verse from Pennsylvania, circa 1900.

COLEMAN BARKS (b. 1937) has been working for twenty-seven years with Persian scholars to bring the poetry of Jelaluddin Rumi over from Farsi into American English. His free-verse translations have appeared in many books. Two collections of his own poems have also come out recently— *Tentmaking: Poems and Prose Paragraphs* and *Club: Granddaughter Poems*. Barks is the recipient of a grant from the National Endowment for the Arts and the Georgia Commission for the Arts. He is retired now from university teaching and lives in Athens, Georgia.

About "Becoming Milton," Barks writes, "When my airport driver Milton tells the story of his son's experience in the (first) Gulf War, he reveals his own careful attention to detail (no matter how horrific), which is one of the ways of love, and work, he has taught his son.

"In the video-game techno-carnage of our time, war has

nothing to do with becoming a warrior. Tom returns sickened and cynical. Very few poems came out of Desert Storm. This one is just two noncombatants talking on a night drive down I-85 from Spartanburg to Athens (famous warring city-states!). In that cubicle of unknowing, our voices merge with wondering why there isn't some other way: to settle conflict, to get more kindness and craftmanship in our life, some way not to do such wretched damage. Surely the most urgent human predicament.

"So Tom's integrity survives in the quality of his carpentry, alongside his father's level, heartbreaking assessments. Outside the poem, my own amazement grows for how unlikely it seems we'll stop this murderous, oil-driven folly anytime soon."

SELECTED READING

The Essential Rumi (translator, poems; HarperSanFrancisco)
Tentmaking: Poems and Prose Paragraphs (Maypop Books)

ELLEN BASS's (b. 1947) most recent book of poems, *Mules of Love,* was published by BOA Editions. She's the coeditor of the groundbreaking book *No More Masks!: An Anthology of Poems by Women* and the author of four previous volumes of poetry. Her nonfiction books include *I Never Told Anyone, Free Your Mind,* and *The Courage to Heal,* which has been translated into ten languages. Among her awards for poetry are the Elliston Book Award, the Pablo Neruda Prize, the Larry Levis Prize, and the New Letters Prize. She lives in Santa Cruz, California, where she has taught creative writing since 1974. She can be visited at www.ellenbass.com.

Ellen Bass writes, "It's always easier to blame the other person in difficult relationships. In this poem I attempt to face the qualities in myself that led me to the brink of disaster. After this experience, I felt I understood something I'd never understood before—how a person could be desperate enough to commit a violent act, how the compulsion to get the pain out might lead to inflicting it on someone else. As a poet, I have a deep curiosity about the human experience—including those aspects that are dishonorable. I believe that when we can fully acknowledge these parts of ourselves, we are better able to have compassion for others."

SELECTED READING
Mules of Love (poems; BOA Editions)

VICTOR H. BAUSCH (b. 1945) is a Vietnam veteran (1967–1968), a member of Veterans for Peace, and a member of the National Writers Union. He earned an M.A. in English from California State University, Stanislaus, and a Master's in Library Science from San Jose State University. He is a reference librarian at Monterey Public Library. Bausch's poetry and prose poems have appeared in various small-press magazines, anthologies, and e-zines.

About his poem Bausch says, "'What They Wanted' is my revenge poem for being drafted and sent to Vietnam. Years later I read the 1954 Geneva Accords and the Pentagon Papers. The final declaration of the Geneva Accords divided Vietnam temporarily into two regrouping zones at the seventeenth parallel. The free national elections to be held in July

1956 were to unify the country, not separate it into North Vietnam and South Vietnam. The Pentagon Papers show that all U.S. presidents from Truman to Nixon lied about what they were doing in Vietnam. Over two million civilians were murdered there, countless others in Laos and Cambodia. Unfortunately, the sad truth, as Plato said, is 'only the dead have seen the end of war.'"

WENDELL BERRY (b. 1934) is both a writer and a farmer who makes his home in Kentucky, on his ancestral farm, where he and his family raise crops and livestock. Both his life and his books are based on a connection to place. He believes there's a profound link between the cultivation of land and the cultivation of thought, and that Americans suffer from a lack of such connection and the integrity that comes of it. Berry has authored more than thirty books of poetry, essays, and novels, and is the recipient of fellowships from the Guggenheim and the Rockefeller foundations, a grant from the National Endowment for the Arts, and the Lannan Foundation Award. He has taught at both New York University and the University of Kentucky.

In a poem titled "Some Further Words," Berry expresses the intention for his writing: "My purpose / is a language that can repay just thanks / and honor for those gifts, a tongue / set free from fashionable lies."

SELECTED READING
In the Presence of Fear: Three Essays for a Changed World (Orion Society, 2001)

A Timbered Choir: The Sabbath Poems 1979–1997 (Counterpoint, 1997)

GEORGE BILGERE (b. 1951) is the author of three collections of poetry, and his poems have appeared in such journals as *The Sewanee Review, Poetry,* and *The Kenyon Review.* He grew up in California, and has lived in England, Japan, and Spain. Currently he lives in Cleveland, Ohio, where he teaches modern poetry at John Carroll University.

About the connection between poetry and forgiveness, Bilgere writes, "The act of writing about the things that have always bothered me is a way of making peace with them. I think most of us spend a lot of our adult lives in the futile task of trying to understand our parents. 'Catch' is only one of many poems I've written about my father, a complex man (like all men) who died before I had a chance to know him as an adult. Perhaps the reason I write about him so often is that I'm always making an effort to fill in the blank spaces, to provide a voice for his silence he left me with."

SELECTED READING
Big Bang: Poems (Copper Beech Press)
The Good Kiss: Poems (University of Akron Press)

CATHERINE BOWMAN (b. 1957) was born in El Paso, Texas. She currently lives in Bloomington, Indiana, where she teaches at Indiana University. She is the award-winning author of two collections of poems. Her poems have appeared in four editions of the Best American Poetry series, and in many publications, such as *TriQuarterly, River Styx, The Kenyon Review,* the *Los Angeles Times,* and *The Paris Review.* She is the editor of *Word of Mouth: Poems Featured on NPR's* All Things Considered.

Bowman's poem "No Sorry" began when Sam, the five-year-old son of a friend, asked her if she had a pair of scissors he could borrow. But she didn't have any. Bowman says about the boy's question in *The Best American Poetry 1999,* "For some reason it made me feel kind of dizzy." She wrote the line down, knowing she wanted to use it in a poem. "Although Sam's question was perfectly innocent, I decided to imagine a different speaker, unnamed, who might have a different motive for asking the question, and another speaker, also unnamed, answering back. I imagined them in my head as neighbors that might borrow a cup of sugar or milk, only I decided to replace the sugar and milk with barbed wire and missiles. . . . The media present world events to us in such an abstract, disembodied format—I'm thinking of the [first] Gulf War—that it seems like a game sometimes, something unreal. . . ."

SELECTED READING
1–800–HOT–RIBS (poems; Gibbs Smith)
Rock Farm (poems; Gibbs Smith)
Word of Mouth: Poems Featured on NPR's All Things Considered (editor; Vintage)

GEORGE BRADLEY (b. 1953), in addition to being the author of several volumes of poetry, has been a construction worker, a sommelier, and a writer of advertising copy. He's a member of the New York Fencers Club. His awards include the Cook Prize and the Yale Series of Younger Poets Prize. Bradley also writes screenplays and criticism and is a contributor to such periodicals as *The New Yorker* and *Shenandoah*.

SELECTED READING

Some Assembly Required (poems; Knopf)

The Yale Younger Poets Anthology, Vol. 93 (editor; Yale University Press)

JOHN BREHM's (b. 1955) poems have appeared in *Poetry, The Southern Review,* and *Best American Poetry 1999,* among other publications. He's the author of a chapbook of poetry, and lives in Brooklyn, New York.

On poetry and forgiveness, Brehm writes, "Poetry provides a place where the energies of revenge and forgiveness can come into play and where a playful tension can be established between them. In 'Sea of Faith,' there is a rising anger that reaches its apex and then turns into its opposite, compassion. I hope that this emotional trajectory feels satisfying in the poem because it touches the truth of where anger, or the desire for revenge, will always finally bring us if we let it: to a sense of our shared vulnerability and the knowledge of how much we are like those who infuriate us."

SELECTED READING

The Way Water Moves (poems; Flume Press)

STERLING A. BROWN (1901–1989) was born in Washington, D.C. He earned both his bachelor's and master's degrees from Harvard University. Brown taught at Howard University. His first book of poems, which won him considerable praise, was published when he was thirty-one. A poet of the Harlem Renaissance, his poetry was influenced by jazz, the blues, work songs, and spirituals. The Great Depression made it impossible for Brown to find a publisher for his second book of poetry, so he turned his attention to writing essays and to his career as a teacher. His second book of poems didn't appear until 1975. Brown's work is known for its portraits of African Americans and its use of African-American folklore and contemporary idiom.

SELECTED READING

The Collected Poems of Sterling A. Brown (Michael S. Harper, editor; Triquarterly Books)

Gaius Valerius Catullus (84 B.C.–54 B.C.): Though not many details about the life of the Roman poet Catullus have survived, it is known that he lived wildly. He was born to a wealthy family. His father was friends with Julius Caesar, of whom Catullus later became vocally critical. Much of what is known about him comes from his poetry, which was quite different from most of what was being written in Catullus's time. Instead of writing epic poetry, with its public themes, Catullus used everyday language to write shorter lyrics about personal experiences, often in a voice that was playful, humorous, and sometimes crude. His poems were about real people and events in Rome during a time of much conflict and violence. Only a single manuscript of 116 poems, which was lost and discovered more than once, has survived. In the poem included here, Catullus speaks frankly of the loss of his brother who died at Troy. Catullus's poetry greatly influenced poets who came after him—Horace and Robert Herrick among them. He was thirty years old when he died.

SELECTED READING

The Complete Poetry of Catullus (David D. Mulroy, translator; University of Wisconsin Press)

SANDRA CISNEROS (b. 1954) is a poet, novelist, short-story writer, and essayist. Born in Chicago, the only daughter among seven children, Cisneros earned her B.A. from Loyola University and her M.A. from the Writers' Workshop at the University of Iowa. She has received fellowships from the National Endowment for the Arts and the MacArthur Foundation. Cisneros has taught at many colleges and universities, including the University of California, the University of Michigan, and the University of New Mexico. Her book of short stories, *The House on Mango Street*, was met with much critical acclaim, winning the American Book Award from the Before Columbus Foundation. In her fiction she writes about her heritage, giving voice to Chicano life and culture. Her most recent book is a novel, *Caramelo*. About the language of her new book, *El Andar* magazine says, "*Caramelo* is a cultural experience filled with *recuerdos,* memories, worlds like *la capirucha, canciones de amor* by María Grever, *fotonovelas,* mole, rebozos, *cielitos lindos, camas matrimoniales,* mariachis, chiles, and *muchachas bonitas.*" Cisneros lives in San Antonio, Texas.

LUCILLE CLIFTON (b. 1936), one of America's favorite poets, was born in New York to parents who passed on to her their great appreciation for books. The first person in her family to finish high school, she began college when she was sixteen. Soon after, she married and by her early thirties had six children, all under eight years old. Langston Hughes was the first to publish Clifton's work, which appeared in the anthology *Poetry of the Negro*. Her first book of poems, *Good Times,* was published when she was thirty-nine. Clifton has received many awards, including, in 2000, the National Book Award. She is also the author of more than twenty children's books, including the well-known Everett Anderson series. Clifton's poems bear witness, often tackling difficult subjects—drug abuse, poverty, slavery, and physical abuse. She says, "[S]omeone must be a voice, someone must notice things and see beyond the obvious. If one person speaks, no one can say that they never heard." Clifton currently lives in Maryland, where she is a professor of English at Saint Mary's College. About herself she writes, "Sometimes I am foolish, prone to error, silly, mistaken, and downright bad." But, she says, "You do the best you can. . . ."

The Book of Light (poems; BOA Editions)
Blessing the Boats: New and Selected Poems (BOA Editions)

EMILY DICKINSON (1830–1886) published only seven poems during her lifetime. After her death, 1,700 poems written on scraps of paper, some of which she'd bound into booklets, were discovered. Some were published in a book but heavily edited, the inventive punctuation she used— frequent dashes and capital letters in unexpected places— replaced with conventional punctuation. Dickinson's was a never-before-heard voice. It wasn't until 1955 that her poetry appeared in print as she had written it. Much of her adult life was spent in her family's house in Amherst, Massachusetts. She received visitors there, but rarely welcomed strangers. Dickinson rejected conventional life and religion, but it hardly appears that she was unhappy with her life. When her niece came to visit in her sunny corner room, the poet said to her, "Matty: here's freedom."

Of Dickinson poet Adrienne Rich wrote, "I have come to view her as somehow too strong for her environment, a figure of powerful will, not at all frail or breathless. . . ." Her poetry is startling and complex, a window into her rich inner life.

SELECTED READING

The Complete Poems of Emily Dickinson (Thomas H. Johnson, editor; Little, Brown and Company)

The Life of Emily Dickinson (by Richard B. Sewall; Harvard University Press)

JOHN DONNE (1572–1631) was born a Roman Catholic at a time when anti-Catholic feeling was at its height in England. He attended Cambridge and Oxford but never took a degree, and for his first forty-three years, lived a life that alternated between destitution and a series of hand-me-down employments from prominent friends. This situation was intensified in 1601 by his secret marriage to Ann More, the niece of Sir Thomas Edgerton's wife, at a time when Donne was serving Edgerton as personal secretary. Not only did the marriage lose him his position, he was briefly thrown into prison by his wife's father, who disapproved of his Catholic background. For the next twelve years he and his growing family endured a number of low-level positions. But when he publicly renounced Catholicism in 1611, and not only became an Anglican but took holy orders in 1615 at the age of forty-three, his fortunes changed. In six years he was named dean of St. Paul's and was one of the most revered preachers in the kingdom. However, his wife, who had suffered through the years of hardship, and whom Donne loved uncompromisingly, did not live to see his fame.

Poet Morton Marcus writes, "Donne's poetry, as well as the work of those he influenced, was a reaction against the simple, emotional, highly decorated Elizabethan lyrics with their clichéd imagery. In contrast, Donne's poems are based on 'wit,' which in the seventeenth century meant a quick insight expressed in a bold comparison. His writing was highly original, and at times outlandish. It used extended metaphors (called 'conceits'). Donne's poems are written in a conversational style, using images from everyday life."

SELECTED READING
The Complete Poetry and Selected Prose of John Donne
(Charles M. Coffin, editor; Modern Library)

STEPHEN DUNN (b. 1939) was born in New York City. He earned an M.A. in creative writing. Dunn has been a professional basketball player, written advertising copy, worked as an editor, and taught as a professor of creative writing. The author of several books of poems, in 2001 he won the Pulitzer Prize for poetry. Dunn's other honors include the Academy Award in literature from the American Academy of Arts and Letters, the James Wright Prize, and fellowships from the National Endowment for the Arts and the New Jersey State Council on the Arts. He has taught poetry and creative writing at many universities and is currently Richard Stockton College of New Jersey Distinguished Professor of Creative Writing. Dunn lives in Port Republic, New Jersey.

SELECTED READING
Different Hours (poems; W. W. Norton & Co.)
New and Selected Poems: 1974–1994 (W. W. Norton & Co.)

FAIZ AHMED FAIZ (1911–1984) was born in Sialkot (which became a part of Pakistan at the time of Partition in 1947, when the English created Pakistan by dividing off a portion of India). For decades before his death in 1984 he was the most distinguished and most beloved poet in the subcontinent. Though first of all a poet, Faiz was also a teacher, a Sufi, an editor of the *Pakistan Times,* and a celebrated radical who was imprisoned in 1951, sentenced to death, and placed in solitary confinement. Four years later he was released. He went into voluntary exile after the dictator Zia ul Haq sentenced the previous prime minister, Zulfikar Ali Bhutto, to death by hanging, and carried out the sentence. Faiz lived in exile in Beirut, where he edited the international literary magazine *Lotus*, then later went home to Pakistan and died soon afterward in the place of his birth.

Naomi Lazard worked with Faiz for five years, translating his poems. She has published six books of poetry, a book for children, and short stories. Her poetry has appeared in many journals. She has received two National Endowment for the Arts Fellowships for poetry.

About poetry, revenge, and forgiveness, Lazard writes, "Poetry can have nothing to do with revenge at least as far as it is understood. Revenge is a striking out, a retaliation. Poetry is a cry from the vulnerable spirit, the giving over, sharing, allowing others to experience the poet as she experiences herself."

SELECTED READING

The Rebel's Silhouette: Selected Poems (Agha Shahid Ali, translator; University of Massachusetts Press)

ROBERT FROST (1874–1963) began writing poetry in high school, and he first published a poem when he was twenty. Though Frost attended college—both Dartmouth and Harvard—he didn't earn a formal degree. After he left school, he worked as a teacher, cobbler, and editor. By the 1920s he was the most celebrated poet in the United States. In 1961 he was invited by President Kennedy to read one of his poems at Kennedy's inauguration. Frost's wife, Elinor, was a major inspiration of his poetry, much of which focused on the life and landscape of New England. He was friends with Ezra Pound, who helped to promote and publish his work. Frost's awards include four Pulitzer Prizes. He taught poetry at universities for many years.

In a 1918 interview, Frost said, "One critic says that I make my imagination too concrete. As if imagination could be made too concrete! Poetic diction is all wrong. Words must be the ordinary words that we hear about us, to which the imagination must give an iridescence. Then only are words really poetic."

SELECTED READING

The Poetry of Robert Frost (Edward C. Lathem, editor; Henry Holt and Company)

Robert Frost: A Life (biography by Jay Parini; Henry Holt)

LOUISE GLÜCK (b. 1943), the United States poet laureate for 2003–04, was born in New York City and educated at Sarah Lawrence College and Columbia University. She has taught at many universities. Her awards include a Rockefeller Fellowship, a grant from the National Endowment for the Arts, and a PEN award for nonfiction. About Glück, critic Helen Vendler said, "Her poems . . . have achieved the unusual distinction of being neither 'confessional' nor 'intellectual.' "

SELECTED READING
Ararat (poems; HarperCollins Publishers, Inc.)
Vita Nova (poems; Ecco Press)

ABRAHAM HALPERN (1914–1985) is the translator of "Song from a Quechan myth." The song was sung in the Yuma language, also known as Quechan. The Yuma people are from southern California. Halpern spent considerable time studying this language and produced a grammar of it as a doctoral thesis. No information is known about the singer of the song.

In his book, *Surviving Through the Days: Translations of Native California Stories and Songs: A California Indian Reader,* Herbert W. Luthin writes about Native California oral literatures: "Most California cultures had no restrictions on who could perform the verbal art. Men and women alike sang songs, recited myths, and told stories. . . . Songs by and large are closely tied to their occasions—that is, you wouldn't normally sing a hunting song except in the proper context of hunting, or a ceremonial song apart from its attendant ceremony—but there are so many different kinds of songs, and song contexts, that few aspects of life are devoid of the opportunity for singing them."

SELECTED READING
Surviving Through the Days: Translations of Native California Stories and Songs: A California Indian Reader (Herbert W. Luthin, editor; University of California Press)

HEINRICH HEINE (1797–1856) was twenty-nine years old when a collection of his poetry was published. He was not paid anything for the book, and neither he nor the publisher had great expectations for its success. Several years later, however, *Book of Songs* became the most famous book of German poetry in the world. The poem published here, "Envenomed are my songs," is from that book, made up mostly of poems of unrequited love. Heine is best known for his early lyric poems. More of his poems have been set to music than those of any other poet.

Heine was a German poet of Jewish origin, who was more highly regarded in France, England, and America than at home. He lived during a time of major social and political upheaval. The French Revolution and the Napoleonic wars greatly influenced his poetry and thinking.

During his lifetime, however, he was best known for his witty prose, political journals, and caustic satires. This writing gave him a controversial reputation but made him quite popular among the more enlightened of Europe's intelligentsia. His liberal views and his attacks on religion were often censored. In Germany he was scorned and discriminated against for his writing and because of his being Jewish. Later, the Nazis insisted that the poet's songs should be marked "author unknown" in poetry collections. Heine's work was valued by such important figures as Karl Marx, Rainer Maria Rilke, and Sigmund Freud.

Although Heine's poetry would later become immensely successful, and though he did establish himself as an author on the German literary scene, he was unable to make a living writing poetry. In order to have a career in civil service, a profession closed to Jews in his time, Heine converted to Protestantism. He pursued a law degree, traveled thoughout Europe, and unsuccessfully attempted a career in politics. Heine suffered both financially and physically. He died in Paris, where he'd been a central figure of the literary scene. And on his deathbed he said, "God will pardon me, it is His trade."

SELECTED READING
Songs of Love & Grief: A Bilingual Anthology (Walter W. Arndt, translator; Northwestern University Press)

GEORGE HERBERT (1593–1633) was a poet and writer. His father died when he was only three, leaving his mother with ten children. She was determined to educate and raise her children as loyal Anglicans. Herbert attended Westminster School and later won a scholarship to Trinity College. He became an orator, representing Trinity at public occasions. Herbert was elected as a representative to Parliament. He later became a minister for the Church of England and spent the rest of his life as the rector of the parish of Bemerton and Fugglestone. While there, he preached and wrote poetry. On his deathbed he sent a poetry manuscript to a friend, asking him to publish the poems only if he thought they might benefit "any dejected poor soul." He died of consumption in 1633 at the age of forty, and his book *The Temple,* which was met with great public acclaim, was published in the same year. Herbert's poems are characterized by a deep religious devotion, precision, metrical agility, and ingenious use of conceit.

SELECTED READING
The Complete English Works (Everyman's Library)

Robert Herrick's (1591–1674) poetry was lauded for its lyricism and condemned for being obscene. But it wasn't until the latter half of the twentieth century that he became recognized as one of the most accomplished poets of his time, having been long dismissed as a minor poet. When Herrick was a baby, his father committed suicide. His mother never remarried. Herrick's father became a significant figure in much of his poetry. The poet studied at Saint John's College and then Trinity Hall in Cambridge. Herrick later became a vicar in Devonshire.

Herrick followed Ben Jonson's prescription for writing well—to read the ancient Greek and Roman poets, to impose his own sensibilities on themes borrowed from classic poetry, and to revise. He wrote, "Better 'twere my Book were dead, / Than to live not perfected."

SELECTED READING
Robert Herrick (poems; Everyman Paperback Classic)

William Heyen (b. 1940) was born and raised in New York. He received his Ph.D. from Ohio University and is Professor of English/Poet in Residence Emeritus at SUNY Brockport. Heyen is the recipient of fellowships from the National Endowment for the Arts and the Guggenheim Foundation. His poems, articles, and essays have appeared in many literary magazines and journals, including *Poetry* and *The New Yorker.* He has edited several anthologies.

In the preface to his anthology *September 11, 2001: American Writers Respond,* Heyen writes, "Such mania evokes new dimensions of fear and realization and commitment in us, disrupts and challenges the romantic American imagination as perhaps never before, and demands from us a different retaliation, an intricate move toward world justice for each star or stripe on every Old Glory now or to come."

SELECTED READING
Diana, Charles, & the Queen (poems; BOA Editions)
Pig Notes & Dumb Music: Prose on Poetry (BOA Editions)
September 11, 2001: American Writers Respond (poems and prose; Etruscan Press)

TED HUGHES (1930–1998), a poet laureate of England, began writing poems as a teenager. He claimed his work was influenced by his father's telling of his experiences fighting in World War I and his own early life on the dramatic landscape of the moors in England. During his childhood, he began careful observation of nature. Hughes studied at Cambridge University. In addition to poetry for adults, he published several books of verse for children as well as translations and a volume of prose. In 1998 Hughes received the Whitbread Prize. In 1956 he met the American poet Sylvia Plath, who encouraged him in his writing. They married later that year and had two children. Following their decision to separate, Plath committed suicide, and for thirty-five years Hughes didn't publish poetry on the subject of their relationship. His final collection, *The Birthday Letters,* documents his relationship with Plath.

Perhaps the most famous subject of his poetry is "Crow," from which the poem here comes, an amalgam of god, bird, and man. He used this being in his work to express his thoughts about good and evil. Of Hughes's work critic John Bayley writes, "Hughes had the same spontaneity of craft, which came from some inner joy in the ceremonial powers of poetry."

SELECTED READING
The Birthday Letters (poems; Farrar, Straus & Giroux)
Selected Poems, 1957–1994 (Farrar, Straus & Giroux)

X. J. KENNEDY (b. 1929) writes for three very different audiences—children; college students, for whom he writes textbooks; and adults, whom he refers to as "that small band of people who still read poetry." Kennedy's given first name is Joseph, but when he began to publish—his first poems appeared in *The New Yorker*—he chose a pseudonym, tired of being teased about being related to John F. Kennedy. His first book of poems won him the Lamont Award of the Academy of American Poets. Together with his wife, Kennedy compiled a now well-known anthology of children's poetry, *Knock at a Star: A Child's Introduction to Poetry.* He's also written young-adult fiction. He's received much recognition and many awards for his work, including a fellowship from the National Council on the Arts and Humanities, a Shelley Memorial Award, and a Guggenheim Fellowship. Kennedy has given more than two hundred readings in the United States and England, and has appeared on radio, on television, and in grade schools. About his work for children he says, "I'm not just a versifier; don't try to persuade children that everything is sweetness and light. . . . The face of a world, however imaginary, has to have a few warts, if a child is going to believe in it; and it must wear an occasional look of foolishness or consternation. It also needs, I suspect, a bit of poetry, and a dash of incredible beauty and enchantment, if possible."

X. J. Kennedy writes, " 'Curse on a Thief' springs from an incident that actually happened. My nephew Paul, an avid fisherman, suffered the loss of his cherished tackle box one day when he left it for a moment on a dock in Fox Lake, Wisconsin. Paul is a gentle man, a forgiving Christian, and wouldn't have uttered such a curse in a million years, so I felt I had to do it for him. In the vehemence of this curse, I was inspired by those Irish and Scottish poets of the Middle Ages who wrote many such scathing poems. It was said that a Celtic bard possessed supernatural powers: his language might scorch the skin off an enemy's back. In modern times, Irish poets have written curses with tongue in cheek, that is, with intent to be funny. James Stephens, to name one, has a poem called 'A Glass of Beer,' in which an old barfly utters a curse upon a barmaid who refused him a drink ('May she marry a ghost and bear him a kitten!') In Stephens's poem and in mine, as I trust you'll notice, the size of the curse is out of all proportion to the size of the crime."

SELECTED READING

Knock at a Star: A Child's Introduction to Poetry (coeditor; Little, Brown and Company)

The Lords of Misrule: Poems 1992–2001 (Johns Hopkins University Press)

ALISON LUTERMAN (b. 1958): Her first book of poems, *The Largest Possible Life*, was published in 2001, and her second book is forthcoming. In addition to poetry, she writes essays and stories, and she is working on a play, *Saying Kaddish with My Sister*, which is about forgiveness and reconciliation between family members and between Jews and Palestinians. Luterman is active in a Jewish-Palestinian dialogue group and is a neighborhood peace activist. She teaches poetry in schools and studies improvisational theater.

Luterman says, "No forgiveness without empathy. No empathy without the imagination. Those of us who work closely with imaginative language know that it is through the alchemy of passion that the solid lead of anger and old wounds melts into the gold of art."

SELECTED READING

The Largest Possible Life (poems; Cleveland State University Press)

MORTON MARCUS (b. 1936) is the author of nine volumes of poetry and one novel. More than four hundred of his poems have been published in literary journals, and his work has appeared in more than seventy-five anthologies in the United States, Europe, and Australia. His newest books are *Moments Without Names: New & Selected Prose Poems* and *Bear Prints,* his collected verse poems. In 1999 Marcus was recognized as Artist of the Year in Santa Cruz, California.

Marcus writes, "I was thinking about guilt. It was a warm summer day in the mountains. I have no idea why I was thinking about guilt. Maybe because the day was so exquisite I couldn't conceive of anyone feeling guilty about anything, or maybe I was feeling guilty about enjoying the day so much. My musings soon led me to the notion that so many of us burden ourselves with guilt over many things that soon we become grotesques, mental cripples. 'Forgiveness' happened exactly as the poem describes, and I leave it to the reader to ruminate on the causes of the man's action. How do we come to hate ourselves so much? Not that we don't need redemption and many times should, in all humility, realize our trespasses against each other, but there was in this case a reaction that seemed to go beyond sanity. Then again, I still wonder if he needed that sense of overwhelming guilt in order to survive the trauma he had endured or may have committed. How do you envision you would endure horrors beyond your imagining?"

SELECTED READING

Bear Prints (poems; Creative Arts Book Company)

Moments Without Names: New & Selected Prose Poems (White Pine Press)

Shouting Down the Silence: Verse Poems, 1988–2001 (Creative Arts Book Company)

KAT MEADS (b. 1951) was born and raised in North Carolina. She received a B.A. in psychology and an M.F.A. in creative writing. Meads is the author of eight books and chapbooks of poetry, fiction, and essays. Her most recent poetry collection is *Quizzing the Dead*. Her short plays have been produced in New York, California, and the Midwest.

Her writing has appeared in many literary journals. Most recently she received a 2002–2003 California Artist Fellowship in fiction and a 2003 National Endowment for the Arts Award in literature.

Kat Meads writes, "The first shattering loss of my life was the death of my pet. Mixed with the overwhelming grief was a sense of cruel injustice: Why me? Why my dog? My poem 'Dogs' was an attempt to re-create not only the hurt and rage, but also the vengefulness I felt toward this random adult, who had, in an instant, deprived me of a beloved companion. I wrote many drafts of the poem, and each revision never failed to reactivate my desire to make poor Edward Sanderlin (long dead himself) pay for his crime."

SELECTED READING

Born Southern and Restless (essays; Duquesne University Press)
Not Waving (short stories; Livingston Press)
Quizzing the Dead (poems; Pudding House Press)

SEMEZDIN MEHMEDINOVIC (b. 1960) was born in Bosnia. He graduated from the University of Sarajevo in 1983, at a time when the former Yugoslavia was already in crisis. Mehmedinovic was a dissident, and as the authorities had no tolerance for opposition, he was banned from employment for nine years. He continued to work as a writer and performing artist, however, publishing his first book of poetry, which was selected as the best book of poetry in Bosnia in 1983–1984. Mehmedinovic also worked as an editor and columnist for several magazines, including *Fantom*

Slobode (*Phantom of Freedom*), which he founded and published with the the help of artist friends who shared his vision of creating a forum for young unknown writers and introducing the work of foreign authors. Two issues of the publication were banned by the government. In 1990 Mehmedinovic published his second book of poetry. When the war in Bosnia began in 1992, he and his family remained as "internally displaced" persons in besieged Sarajevo. Together with his friends he started a new magazine, *Dani* (*Days*), in an effort to support the spirit of democratic rule and pluralism during what became a systematic genocide against his compatriots. *Dani* was printed under the worst conditions, in a city without food, electricity, running water, or printing supplies, under constant attack by Serb forces. Its staff sold the issues on the streets under aerial bombardment, mortar attack, shelling, and sniper fire through three and a half years of war. *Dani* is still considered the best magazine in Bosnia. In 1993 Mehmedinovic coedited a collection of stories and poems written by Sarajevo's citizens. The following year, along with five other Bosnian writers, he received the Hellman-Hammett Award for persistence in preserving democracy in the midst of war. He then worked as an editor in radio and continued to publish articles in newspapers in Bosnia and abroad, some of which aroused the wrath of authorities who banned him from the Bosnian media and denied him permission to leave Sarajevo. In 1995 he went to Zagreb, in Croatia, at the request of his family, who were concerned for his security, and there published a second, revised version of *Sarajevo Blues*, which had first come out in 1992. Mehmedinovic arrived in the United

States as a political refugee in 1996, and currently lives in Virginia. His articles, poems, and essays have been translated and published in leading European and American newspapers and magazines.

Mehmedinovic writes about his poem "Hero": "The question of revenge or forgiveness is in direct connection with the way one rids oneself of trauma. War is the consequence of greed and politics of indifference, and the time after the war is marked with politically determined oblivion. When traumatic memories are suppressed, frustration increases and solutions may be found through revenge. In the way today's societies are arranged, there's no space for dealing with painful memories such as those expressed in 'Hero,' and those caused by loss of one's family. Because of that, forgiveness, like psychological purgation of trauma, appears impossible."

SELECTED READING

Nine Alexandrias (poems; City Lights Books)
Sarajevo Blues (poems; City Lights Books)

TONI MIROSEVICH (b. 1952) is the author of two books of poetry. Her fiction, poetry, and essays have appeared in *The Kenyon Review, The Progressive, The Best of Web del Sol, Best American Travel Writing 2002,* and other literary journals. Mirosevich's literary awards include an Academy of American Poets Award, *San Francisco Bay Guardian* Poetry Prize, and Americas Review Poetry Prize. In 1999 she was the national recipient of the Astraea Foundation Emerging Lesbian Writer in Fiction Award. She is an assistant professor of creative writing at San Francisco State University.

Mirosevich writes, "The poem 'Hygiene' attempts to raise questions about the desire for revenge (Who could have foreseen the boy's return to the gas station to commit the murder?), the need for forgiveness (Who will forgive the boy for the senseless murder? Who will forgive the poet who witnessed the preceding events of the boy's life and wrote a poem but did not in other ways intervene with the course of events?), and the issue of culpability. As poets, when we are forced to attend to the world around us, to the lives around us, what are our responsibilities as witnesses? I have far too many questions and very few answers. When I write poetry, questions grow at an alarming rate."

SELECTED READING
The Rooms We Make (poems; Firebrand Books)
Trio (poems; Specter Press)

NAOMI SHIHAB NYE (b. 1952) was born in St. Louis to an American mother and a Palestinian father. She published her first poem when she was seven. When she was fourteen her family moved to Jerusalem, and there she attended one year of high school. Her family then moved to San Antonio, Texas, where she still lives. Nye received her B.A. in 1974. In addition to writing poetry, she is the author of books for children and the editor of several poetry anthologies for young people. Nye is the recipient of many awards, including four Pushcart Prizes, a Jane Addams Children's Book Award, the Paterson Poetry Prize, and many Notable Book and Best Book citations from the American Library Association.

In an essay in the *Alan Review,* Nye discusses her inspiration for writing: "How did other people live their lives? Just a sense of so many other worlds out there, beginning with the next house on my own street, gave me a great energy." Nye sees a connection between poetry and empathy, and writes, "Isn't this where empathy begins? Other countries stop seeming quite so 'foreign' or inanimate, or strange, when we listen to the intimate voices of their citizens."

SELECTED READING
Fuel (poems; BOA Editions)
19 Varieties of Gazelle: Poems of the Middle East (Greenwillow Books)

KENNETH PATCHEN (1911–1972) was born in Ohio. From the time he was twelve, he kept a diary and was an avid reader of, among other authors, Dante, Melville, and Shakespeare. He was a migrant worker in both the United States and Canada. When he was twenty-one his first poem was published in the *New York Times.* Patchen is the author of more than forty books of poetry, prose, and drama. In 1942, he published *The Dark Kingdom,* a limited edition of seventy-five copies; he hand-painted each cover individually. Kenneth Patchen and his wife, Miriam, were quite in love, and he wrote her many poems. Of her husband, Miriam Patchen wrote, "Kenneth Patchen was a poet; he was that all the time. He is that still. That is what is meant by 'poet.' The poetry never stops working if it is real." Patchen suffered from a severe spinal ailment that caused him nearly constant pain. His own experience of pain deepened his awareness of the suffering of others. A care and tenderness for people and love for the world fills his work. His was a poetry sensitive to the great issues of humanity—peace and war. Patchen said, "It is not advisable to cheat that which has no other stake than the deeps and brights of all men." His poetry creates a kind of sanctuary that honors the imagination. Patchen wrote, "Any thought or action which injures the human imagination is evil."

SELECTED READING

The Collected Poems of Kenneth Patchen (W. W. Norton)
What Shall We Do Without Us? (poem paintings; Sierra Club Books)

MOLLY PEACOCK (b. 1947) was born in New York and currently lives in both Ontario, Canada, and New York City. She is the author of five books of poems and a book about poetry. Peacock was the president of the Poetry Society of America for several years. She's a contributing writer for *House & Garden*.

About her poem, Peacock writes, "I occupy dangerous ground, the terrain of autobiography and formal design." She's interested in how feeling and form are related. "Structure of line, sound, and vocabulary, combined with the storyteller's art of delaying experience to replicate the terrible tensions of real time passing, let me make art of what happens to me, as I think in some way all poets have been doing since the days of cuneiform."

Cornucopia: New and Selected Poems, 1975–2002 (W. W. Norton)

How to Read a Poem . . . and Start a Poetry Circle (Riverhead Books)

Poetry in Motion: 100 Poems from the Subways and Buses (editor; W. W. Norton)

LILLA CABOT PERRY (1848–1933) was an impressionist painter. Having come from a distinguished Boston family and having not received formal art training until she was thirty-six, it was unlikely she'd become a professional painter. However, that's what she did. During her lifetime, Perry had a solid reputation for both her painting and her poetry. And by selling her paintings, she was able to supplement her husband's income. She was befriended by and studied with Claude Monet. Perry's work is now held by the National Museum of Women in the Arts in Washington, D.C., and the Hunter Museum of American Art in Chattanooga, Tennessee.

EZRA POUND (1885–1972), an Idaho native, graduated from college, taught for two years, then hastened to Europe. There he became interested in poetry from Asia and initiated a movement called Imagism, inspired by classical Chinese and Japanese poetry's attention to clarity and economy of language, not rhyme and meter. He was an extremely prolific and experimental writer. His later poetry was dedicated to a form of epic poetry he called *The Cantos*. His work had an enormous effect on other writers, including William Carlos Williams, Ernest Hemingway, and James Joyce. Pound is known also for his translations of poetry. He lived in various countries in Europe. After settling in Italy, he became involved in fascist politics. Upon returning to the United States in 1945, he was arrested on charges of treason for broadcasting fascist propaganda by radio to the United States during World War II. He was acquitted a year later, but declared mentally ill and committed to a hospital. While there, the jury of the prestigious Bollingen–Library of Congress Award chose to overlook Pound's politics and awarded him their prize for the *Pisan Cantos*. He returned to Italy in 1958, where he lived until his death in 1972.

SELECTED READING

The Cantos (New Directions Press)

The Collected Early Poems of Ezra Pound (New Directions Press)

SARAH RABKIN (b. 1957), a former high-school science teacher and question-and-answer columnist, teaches writing in the Environmental Studies Department at the University of California, Santa Cruz. She also leads outdoor workshops on keeping illustrated field journals and freelances as an editor and writing coach.

Sarah Rabkin says, "I wrote this poem a year after the breakup of a brief but intense love affair. I had left other relationships before, but this was the first time I had been 'dumped.' I knew I had recovered when this and two other playful poems emerged in the space of a week or two. The others leaned toward forgiveness, but 'Wheels'—my first and only revenge poem—was deliciously mean. Having scratched that shiny paint with my pen, so to speak, I no longer felt the urge to do it with my key."

TIM REYNOLDS (b. 1937) was named in 1965 by *Harper's* magazine as one of the four poets under thirty-five considered the best in America. However, today little is known about this author of several collections of poetry who, instead of pursuing a poetry career, chose to travel around the world. Reynolds's memoir, *What Ever Happened,* chronicles his travels, including meetings with such poets as e. e. cummings, Robert Frost, and Ezra Pound.

SELECTED READING
What Ever Happened (memoir; If Publishing)

CHARLES REZNIKOFF (1894–1976) was born in Brooklyn, New York, to Russian Jewish immigrant parents who had fled the pogroms. Reznikoff was a precocious student, graduating three years ahead of his class. He earned a law degree, but practiced for only a short time because he wanted to concentrate on writing. Reznikoff's first book of poetry was published in 1918. He supported himself by working a series of writing and editing jobs. Throughout the 1930s, Reznikoff gained recognition as one of the principal proponents of Objectivism, a modernistic form of poetry. A group of poets established the Objectivist Press and published three of Reznikoff's books. He also published several prose works and a number of plays. Reznikoff lived most of his life in New York City.

Reznikoff's poem published here, "I Will Write Songs Against You," is actually a small part of a long poem that is somewhat surreal—part love poem, part exploration of time—and it looks at how people go their own separate ways in life. The poem is full of surprising and beautiful lines, such as "the day's brightness dwindles into stars."

SELECTED READING

Poems 1918–1936: The Complete Poems of Charles Reznikoff (Seamus Cooney, editor; Black Sparrow Press)

Charles Reznikoff: The Man and Poet (Milton Hindus, editor; National Poetry Foundation)

MURIEL RUKEYSER (1913–1980) was born in New York City. As a young adult she witnessed events that strongly impacted her life and poetry—the Scottsboro trial in Alabama, the Gauley Bridge tragedy in West Virginia, and the civil war in Spain. The violence and injustice in the United States and abroad led her to write poetry of social protest. Rukeyser felt a deep responsibility to respond to injustice through poetry, and was particularly concerned with inequalities of sex, race, and class. In her poetry she frequently wrote about her own emotional experiences but put them in the context of a political or social event. Rukeyser was a visionary—she wished the world to be united by love, and this was fervently expressed in her poetry.

In 1976 American poet Sharon Olds took a class from

Rukeyser. Olds recalls her saying, "No one wants to read poetry. No one wants to! You have to make it impossible for them to put the poem down, impossible for them to stop reading it." In order to write poetry that would demand that attention from a reader, she said, "Your whole life, your whole attention, [must be brought] to the moment of the poem. Everything. That is the secret."

SELECTED READING
The Life of Poetry (nonfiction; Paris Press)
A Muriel Rukeyser Reader (Jan Heller Levi, editor; W. W. Norton)

WILLIAM SHAKESPEARE (c. 1564–1616) was born in England to middle-class parents, the third child and first son of eight children. He was probably educated at the King Edward IV Grammar School in Stratford, where he learned Latin and a little Greek and read the Roman dramatists. At eighteen, he married Anne Hathaway, a woman several years his senior, and they raised two daughters. Shakespeare is the world's most famous and respected playwright. His plays were performed in the Globe Theatre, the most famous theater of its time, where people of all different classes would come to the theater. Only eighteen of his thirty plays were published during his lifetime. A complete collection of his works did not appear until 1623, several years after his death. Nonetheless, his achievements were recognized by his contemporaries. He was a master at creating plays that could be understood and appreciated on multiple levels. Shakespeare's sonnets were written between 1593 and 1601, but not published until 1609. His book *Shakespeare's Sonnets* consisted of 154 sonnets, all written in the form of three quatrains and a couplet, a style that is now recognized as Shakespearean.

SELECTED READING
Complete Poems of Shakespeare (Random House)
The Complete Works of William Shakespeare (Library of Congress Classic)

BARRY SPACKS (b. 1931) calls himself a lifelong freelance editor, whose work has appeared in *The Atlantic Monthly* and *The New Yorker*. He is the author of seven collections of poetry. His writing also appears in many journals and a variety of e-zines. Spacks was a Fulbright Scholar from 1956 to 1957. He was awarded the Commonwealth Club of California's Poetry Medal. He's a professor at the University of California, Santa Barbara, and a student of Tibetan Buddhism.

SELECTED READING
Spacks Street: New and Selected Poems (Johns Hopkins University Press)
A Private Reading (compact disc; WC Productions)

EDMUND SPENSER (c. 1552–1599) was educated by a teacher who believed in giving his students a strong background in the classics and who encouraged them to become involved in music and drama. This gave Spenser the perfect start for becoming a poet. He began writing and publishing poetry before entering college. He wrote sonnets, lyric poetry, translations, epics, allegories, pastoral poetry, essays, and romances. He was hailed as "the Prince of Poets" in his time. In his book *Lives of the Poets,* Michael Schmidt writes, "Spenser follows, as Milton was to do, the Virgilian pattern for becoming a Great Poet. First you write your eclogues, then your georgic, then your epic." Imagine following such a proscribed formula nowadays! As different as their poetry was, Spenser considered himself to be Chaucer's heir. His goal was to enrich England's culture, to help create a poetry that was uniquely English in all ways—religion, politics, history, custom, and language. His most important work was *The Faerie Queene,* which he wrote to glorify Queen Elizabeth. The poet Sir Walter Ralegh arranged for Spenser to present it to the queen, who was so happy with what he wrote she gave him a pension. Spenser was well loved by his English countrymen.

SELECTED READING

The Faerie Queene (Penguin Classics)
The Shorter Poems of Edmund Spenser (Penguin Classics)

WILLIAM STAFFORD (1914–1993) was one of our most prolific and celebrated American poets, the author of more than fifty books. He was a witness for peace and for honesty, recognizing in his writing that "justice will take us millions of intricate moves." Stafford was a professor at Lewis & Clark College for many years and taught poetry in many places around the world. He received the National Book Award. As a conscientious objector during World War II, he began a practice of writing before dawn each day. Stafford was known for his generosity to other writers and readers. After serving as Consultant in Poetry to the Library of Congress in 1970, he was named Oregon's Poet Laureate in 1975. He died at his home in Oregon in 1993.

SELECTED READING

The Darkness Around Us Is Deep: Selected Poems of William Stafford (Robert Bly, editor; HarperPerennial)

Writing the Australian Crawl: Views on the Writer's Vocation (University of Michigan Press)

MARIAHADESSA EKERE TALLIE (b. 1973), New York–born poet and performer, is currently hard at work on her first fiction collection. Her poetry has been anthologized in several collections. A nomad at heart, Tallie divides her time between Amsterdam, New York City, and just about any other inspiring place she can get a cheap ticket to.

Tallie says, "I wrote the poem while washing dishes and listening to a new CD. A song came on where the woman sounded as though she was chanting a broken heart. So I put the dishes down and wrote the poem in what I imagined to be her voice."

About poetry and forgiveness she writes, "Poetry, writing in general, is always a part of my healing process; I think forgiveness and healing go hand in hand. I've forgiven many people, including myself, with a poem."

SELECTED READING

Tallie's work appears in the following anthologies:

Bum Rush the Page: A Def Poetry Jam (Random House)

Listen Up!: Spoken Word Poetry (anthology, edited by Zoë Anglesey; One World/Ballantine)
Lest We Forget (CD; Drum FM)

DIANE THIEL (b. 1967) received the Nicholas Roerich Poetry Prize from Story Line Press in 2000 for her book *Echolocations*. She's also the author of a writing guide, *Writing Your Rhythm*. Her work has appeared in *Poetry*, *The Hudson Review*, and *Best American Poetry 1999*. She was a recipient of the Robert Frost and the Robinson Jeffers awards. A major theme in her work is the effect of war and trauma on children and on future generations. Thiel was a Fulbright Scholar for 2001–2002 in Odessa on the Black Sea. She's currently an assistant professor of creative writing at the University of New Mexico. To learn more about her, go to her webpage: www.dianethiel.net.

About her poem, Thiel writes, "Is there some line we cross when we are finally able to forgive, when we might look into the perpetrator's heart and find something other than the darkest spot? What might look like so much anger is filtered through a life—churned, distilled, then stilled. The telling of the story is a crucial step, first to survive, but then to slowly overcome the past. Though we might always carry the burden of that history, we can find ways to wear it differently."

SELECTED READING
Echolocations: Poems (Story Line Press)
Writing Your Rhythm: Using Nature, Culture, Form and Myth (prose; Story Line Press)

PATRICE VECCHIONE (b. 1957) is the author of *Writing and the Spiritual Life: Finding Your Voice by Looking Within* and a book of poems, *Territory of Wind*. She's the editor of two previous anthologies for young adults: *The Body Eclectic* and *Truth & Lies*, which was named one of the Best Books of 2001 by *School Library Journal*. For children, she edited the anthology *Whisper & Shout: Poems to Memorize*. For twenty-five years, Vecchione has taught poetry to children and adults in schools, libraries, and community centers through her program, The Heart of the Word. A frequent speaker on writing as a spiritual practice, she lives in Monterey, California. For more information about her work, she may be contacted at www.patricevecchione.com.

About her poem she writes, "It was a dream. I woke up frightened, wrote it down, closed my journal, and went about my day. But the dream wouldn't leave me alone. Everything I did and thought was tinged by it, disturbingly so. A few days later, I looked at what I'd written down, began the transformation from notes to poem, immersed myself in what I did not want to look at, knew that was the only medicine. Where did the dream come from? A daughter has a difficult relationship with her mother, one that is both loving and tragic. The poem is an attempt to work out some of the weight of it. Dreams and poems can both bring light to what overwhelms and confuses us. Sometimes the only way to tell a story is through the guise of another story."

SELECTED READING

Territory of Wind (poems; Many Names Press)

Truth & Lies: An Anthology of Poems (for young adults, editor; Henry Holt)

Writing and the Spiritual Life: Finding Your Voice by Looking Within (Contemporary/McGraw-Hill)

DEREK WALCOTT (b. 1930) is from Saint Lucia, in the West Indies, and is the son of an African mother and an English father. His first book of poetry was published when he was eighteen. He graduated from the University of the West Indies, and in 1957 he received a fellowship from the Rockefeller Foundation to study American theater. Walcott founded the Trinidad Theater Workshop, and his plays have been produced throughout the United States. He won an Obie Award for his play *Dream on Monkey Mountain*. Walcott is the author of many books of poems, a collection of essays, and several plays. In 1992 he was awarded the Nobel Prize in Literature. In addition he's the recipient of a MacArthur Foundation Award, a Royal Society of Literature Award, and the Queen's Medal for Poetry. He makes his home in Trinidad and teaches one semester of creative writing a year at Boston University.

Derek Walcott has three central allegiances—Caribbean culture, the English language, and his African roots. In his Nobel Prize acceptance speech, Walcott said this of poetry: "There is the buried language and there is the individual vocabulary, and the process of poetry is one of excavation and of self-discovery. Tonally the individual voice is a dialect; it shapes its own accent, its own vocabulary and melody in defiance of an imperial concept of language. . . . Poetry is an island that breaks away from the main."

SELECTED READING
Collected Poems: 1948–1984 (Noonday Press)
Tiepolo's Hound (poems; Farrar, Straus & Giroux)
What the Twilight Says (essays; Farrar, Straus & Giroux)

MARGARET WALKER (1915–1998), the eldest of five children, was born in Birmingham, Alabama. She was a poet, novelist, and essayist who grew up in a family that loved literature. Her grandmother's stories of slave life in rural Georgia, and Walker's own poetry, were recorded in the first journal she received, a gift from her father. She began writing when she was thirteen. At sixteen she had completed high school and begun college. Walker earned both an M.A. and a Ph.D. from the University of Iowa.

She was encouraged in her writing by both Langston Hughes and W. E. B. DuBois. In 1942 Walker was awarded the Yale Series of Younger Poets Award and her book *For My People* was published. It is in that first book that the poem included here originally appeared. She taught at Jackson State University in Mississippi from 1949 until her retirement in 1979.

Walker wrote, "Here in the United States 'Success' . . . is measured in terms of fame and fortune. . . . A creative worker dealing with the fiery lightning of imagination is interested in artistic accomplishment, and I have spent my life seeking this kind of fulfillment."

SELECTED READING
Conversations with Margaret Walker (Maryemma Graham, editor; University Press of Mississippi)

On Being Female, Black and Free: Essays, 1932–1992 (University of Tennessee Press)

This Is My Century: New and Collected Poems (University of Georgia Press)

CHARLES HENRY WEBB (1834–1905) was a humorist, playwright, and newspaper columnist, as well as a banker, a Wall Street broker, and an inventor. The publication of *Moby Dick* temporarily diverted him from his career in journalism; he was inspired by the book to spend more than three years at sea on a single whaling voyage that took him to the South Seas and the Arctic. Upon his return he published humorous verse and articles in newspapers and magazines, and then joined the *New York Times* as a correspondent, columnist, and literary editor. His parodies and satires were also published in two books. Webb was the editor and publisher of Mark Twain's first book.

WALT WHITMAN (1819–1892) began to learn the trade of printing at the age of twelve and worked as a printer in New York until 1836. When he was seventeen, he worked as a teacher in one-room schoolhouses on Long Island. In 1841 he turned to journalism and founded a weekly newspaper, moving to New Orleans a few years later to become the editor of a paper there. It was in New Orleans that Whitman witnessed firsthand the viciousness of slavery manifested in the slave markets of that city, which impacted him greatly. During the Civil War, Whitman worked as a war correspondent and a government clerk and devoted much of his time to caring for the sick and injured soldiers. He would go to the hospitals in Washington, D.C., carrying a knapsack of gifts for the soldiers—fruit, candy, tobacco, books, pencils, and paper. Because his beard was long and white, and he wore a wine-colored suit and carried a full sack, he looked much like Santa Claus. His visits brought the men friendship and comfort; of this period he said, "I only gave myself."

In 1855 Whitman self-published his book *Leaves of Grass*, which consisted of twelve untitled poems and a preface. Whitman's poetry was revolutionary in its time; he liberated poetry—writing in free verse and using rhythmic innovations that were starkly different from the verse conventions of the era, which were marked by strict rhyme schemes and structural patterns. He believed that the purpose of poetry was not beauty for beauty's sake, but that poetry should express some profound truth, that poetry was a kind of knowledge. He wanted to convey "the unspoken meanings of the earth." Of him, Allen Ginsberg wrote, "Whitman was probably the first writer in America who was not ashamed of the fact that his thoughts were as big as the universe." Of himself, Whitman wrote, "I contain multitudes."

During his lifetime, Whitman continued to refine *Leaves of Grass,* publishing several more editions. It is considered a masterpiece of world literature. Through most of his life, he struggled to support himself. The 1882 publication of *Leaves of Grass* gave Whitman enough money to buy a home.

SELECTED READING

Walt Whitman: The Complete Poems (edited by Francis Murphy; Viking Press)

Walt Whitman's America: A Cultural Biography (by David S. Reynold; Vintage Books)

CECILIA WOLOCH (b. 1956), a teacher of poetry and creative writing for more than fifteen years, is the author of three books of poems. She's on the faculty of the M.F.A. Program in Creative Writing at New England College, and is the director of Summer Poetry in Idyllwild, a weeklong celebration of poets and poetry held in southern California each summer. When not in New England or California, Woloch makes her home in Atlanta.

She writes about her poem "Blink": "I began writing this poem while thinking about the childish wish to be transformed, to be beautiful in a saintly or ethereal way, or at least in a way that others recognized as beautiful. As I was writing, I also thought about the cruelty of the standards of beauty, and the cruelty with which those standards are sometimes enforced—as in the kind of name-calling that goes on among children when one looks somehow 'different.' I thought the poem would end up being angry, a revenge poem; and I suppose in some ways it is, because the speaker gets revenge on those standards of beauty, and the standard-bearers, by finding herself beautiful, after all. In the end, it's a poem of forgiveness, too—the speaker's face is forgiven and accepted, and loved, and thus, in fact, transformed."

SELECTED READING
Tsigan: The Gypsy Poem (Cahuenga Press)

GARY YOUNG (b. 1951) is a poet and artist. His book *Braver Deeds* won the Peregrine Smith Poetry Prize. Young is the recipient of fellowships from the National Endowment for the Arts and the National Endowment for the Humanities. His print work is represented in many collections, including the Museum of Modern Art and the Getty Center for the Arts. He is the editor of the Greenhouse Review Press.

Young writes, "My poem is derived from an unexpected revelation: that anger and pain can sometimes bring their opposites, love and forgiveness, into a sharper focus."

SELECTED READING
Braver Deeds (poems; Gibbs Smith)
No Other Life (poems; Creative Arts Books)

PERMISSIONS

INDEX OF AUTHORS

INDEX OF TITLES

INDEX OF FIRST LINES